THE ULTIMATE ON-LINE HOMEWORK HELPER

Other Avon Camelot Books by
Marian Salzman and Robert Pondiscio

KIDS ON-LINE

Coming Soon

GOING TO THE NET:
A GIRL'S GUIDE TO CYBERSPACE

THE ULTIMATE ON-LINE HOMEWORK HELPER

MARIAN SALZMAN & ROBERT PONDISCIO

AN AVON CAMELOT BOOK

The authors and publisher have used their best efforts to research the services and products contained in this book and make no warranty of any kind, expressed or implied, with regard to these services and products.

THE ULTIMATE ON-LINE HOMEWORK HELPER is an original publication of Avon Books. This work has never before appeared in book form.

AVON BOOKS
A division of
The Hearst Corporation
1350 Avenue of the Americas
New York, New York 10019

Copyright © 1996 by Marian Salzman and Robert Pondiscio
Published by arrangement with the authors
Library of Congress Catalog Card Number: 96-23296
ISBN: 0-380-78662-1

First Avon Camelot Printing: September 1996

CAMELOT TRADEMARK REG. U.S. PAT. OFF. AND IN OTHER COUNTRIES, MARCA REGIS-
TRADA, HECHO EN U.S.A.

Printed in the U.S.A.

OPM 10 9 8 7 6 5 4 3 2 1

Contents

Chapter Ten: Stress-Proof Research Papers

Chapter Eleven: The Coolest Online Hangouts

Index

Acknowledgments

Shortly after the publication of *Kids On-Line* last year, I began getting e-mail from kids who wanted to talk about the book, offer suggestions, point out some of their favorite online hangouts, and ask questions.

Last October, I had a memorable exchange of e-mail with a kid on America Online, known to me only as "Randa," who asked me if Marian and I were planning a sequel to *Kids On-Line*. I mentioned that we were thinking about doing a homework helper. "I've heard that you can use the Internet for help on reports and stuff like that, but I can't figure out where you go to get the information," Randa wrote back enthusiastically. "I've been trying to locate any kind of library or anything that would help. It's frustrating because I know there's ENDLESS information and I can't get to it!"

If we had any doubt that there was a need for this book, that just about iced it.

The idea of doing a book to help kids with schoolwork strikes me as important for another reason. So much media coverage of the Internet and kids focuses on the supposed dangers lurking in cyberspace. While safety online is an important concern, it overshadows how useful a computer with access to the Internet or a good online service can be for students. By putting a large number of fun and educational resources under one cover—and explaining how to use them—my hope is that kids and their parents will realize that the Internet might just be the most important revolution in education since the invention of the number-two pencil.

No book writes itself, and special thanks are due to Susan Gregory Thomas, of Time Warner's Pathfinder, who contributed heavily to the World Wide Web chapter, and offered her sharp eyes and keen insights to several others. An enormous debt is owed to Henry "Hal" Rosengarten, coordinator of the Academic Assistance Center on America Online, and his online teaching staff for their generosity in suggesting web sites for the "Subject by Subject" chapter. The indefatigable Ed Gragert of I*EARN introduced us to dozens of students and teachers over the Internet during the writing of this book. Renee Cho of McIntosh & Otis also worked hard on behalf of this project.

Thanks also to Amy Arnold and Margaret Ryan of America Online; Jane Torbica and Debra Young of CompuServe; and especially Scott Kaufman of WOW! who allowed us a sneak preview of the service in time to meet our deadline. Bonnie Bracey of the National Infrastructure Advisory Council was, as always, a patient and helpful resource.

This book would not have been possible without the steady stream of input from hundreds of students and teachers, several of whom deserve special mention for their input, especially Eileen M. Bendixsen and her students at Beers Street Middle School in Hazlet, New Jersey, for participating in the "Great

Info Showdown." Other teachers who were especially helpful were Patti Weeg, Delmar Elementary School, Delmar, Maryland; Luz C. DuBois, Haverstraw Middle School, Haverstraw, New York; Joan Berger, East Hills School, Roslyn, New York; Mary J. Meewes, Oviedo High School, Oviedo, Florida; David Hoffman, Bass Lake Elementary School, Bass Lake, California; Lynne Mass, Abington Friends School, Jenkintown, Pennsylvania; Jane Farris and Pam Wegeng, L'Ouverture Computer Technology Magnet Elementary School, Wichita, Kansas; and Armand Jaques, Woodland High School [Retired], Woodland, California.

And thanks especially to all the kids who shared with us all their favorite online hangouts and web sites, including Joellen Scheider, Abby Greene, Alex Yalen, Tiffinie Gary, Molly Gebrian, Barrett Thornton, Krista Kufs, Marcelle Young, Kerry McCaughan, Timothy Niessen, Rae Kaplan, Kristopher Mason, Natalie Sliwa, Carrie Davis, Matt Woodington, Ken Roberts, Jenna Burrell, and the members of the Teenagers Circle: Gerald Tan, Najah Onn, Corinne Seaton, Joseph Volence, Daniel Peters, Matt Swoboda, and Andris Kalinka.

I hope you enjoy the book.

Robert Pondiscio
RPondiscio@aol.com
June, 1996

P.S. Yep, that's my e-mail address. Drop me a line! I look forward to hearing your questions and comments.

The Future Is Here

"I think that using a computer and modem is very important for kids because computers are rapidly becoming an important part of our everyday lives."

—Kerry McCaughan,
Lost Mountain Middle School
Kennesaw, GA.

BRAVE NEW WORLD

Cyberspace ... online ... E-mail ... the Net ... the Web. Just a year or two ago, most people had never even heard of them. Now these words are on everyone's lips. Ready or not, the digital revolution has already begun changing the way we live, learn, and play.

You don't have to be a computer whiz or a cyber-geek to understand and take part in this revolution. Going online has never been easier. You can now simply point and click your way to the farthest corners of cyberspace. This book will show you how computers and online communications are changing the world and how you can be part of what some people are calling the most important development

in communications since the invention of the printing press.

OK, so people who say big dramatic things about
how the fate of civilization lies in a network of computer cables should probably turn off their computers every now and then and go out and watch a
sunset, smell some flowers, kiss a girl—get a life! The
real problem with people who get totally caught up
in the online world and talk about it like it's the
greatest thing since the invention of the weekend is
that they tend to scare off people like you and me
who think the whole idea of linking the world together by computer sounds a little bit scary and complicated—not to mention a bit dorky. Not to worry.
The most important thing to remember is that there's
no reason to be a computerphobe. Going online is
simple and easy. And once you're there, you really
can discover a whole new world at your fingertips!
It doesn't have to take over your life, either. But it
can make your life—and especially school!—easier.

And that's what this book is for.

We want to show you how your computer can be
used to find almost any fact or figure in just seconds.
By the time you're finished reading this book, we
guarantee that your computer and a modem will become your most important tools for school. That's
because once you know your way around cyberspace, there's almost no limit to the kinds of cool and
useful places you can explore:

- electronic libraries
- up-to-the-minute news and information sources
- electronic user groups, where you can talk with
  experts, teachers, and other kids

- sources of free software for downloading, and lots more.

Let's get started!

IT'S A WIRED WORLD

Unless you've been living in a *very* deep cave for the last few years, you've heard about the Internet. And if you *have* been living in a cave, then why the heck is this the first book you've picked up now that you're back? The Internet is a huge collection of thousands of computer networks—a network of networks—all tied together by high-speed telephone lines. But to describe the Internet in terms of hardware misses the point. What it *is* isn't as important as what it *does*. It's simply a system that allows computers—and computer users—all over the world to talk to one another. The Internet connects millions of people to one another in over one hundred countries, allowing them to use their computers to communicate and share information.

The Internet was "invented" (sort of—it really *evolved*) in 1969. That's when the U.S. Department of Defense started linking a bunch of people and institutions involved in military research via computer—government workers, universities, civilian defense contractors, and other key people. The result was something called ARPANET (Advanced Research Projects Administration Network). It divided and grew over the years. Eventually it was replaced by something called NSFNET (National Science Foundation Net), which was bigger, faster, and easier to tap into than ARPANET. Then, as computers continued to get smaller, faster, and cheaper, you no longer needed a room-sized mainframe computer to be wired. Anybody could become a player on what became known as the Internet. And they have!

Commercial online services like America Online (AOL) and CompuServe are not the same thing as the Internet (more about that later), but the popularity of these services, driven by the huge growth in the number of people buying personal computers, has led to an online explosion. The number of Americans who subscribe to an online information service more than doubled from five million in the winter of 1994 to nearly twelve million in the summer of 1995.

That may sound like just about everyone, but actually there are millions more with computers connected to modems—the device that lets computers talk to one another—who have never even *tried* going online. In early 1996, the telecommunications giant AT&T began offering access to the Internet at bargain prices to its telephone customers. That move seems to guarantee that we are headed toward the day when access to the Internet will be just as common as access to a telephone.

As with a telephone, having access to the Internet and taking advantage of it are two different things. A telephone can be a vital communications link that can bring a fire truck or ambulance to your house in minutes when there's an emergency. Or you can use it to gab for hours with your friends—and everything in between. One thing is certain: Most people with access to the Internet have only begun to scratch the surface of its potential. A survey in 1995 found that only one out of five of all online users have ever ventured out onto the Internet via the World Wide Web. That's like having an entire nation full of people buying Air Jordans and only wearing them to walk the dog. Changing that is an important goal of this book. We want to show you as much of what's out there as possible, so you'll get more out of being online.

TOP SIX REASONS WHY GOING ONLINE WILL MAKE YOU A BETTER STUDENT

That's the bottom line, right? All this gee-whiz stuff about global interconnectedness is sort of cool, but when all is said and done, we're guessing the reason you're reading this book is to get better grades. Here are six reasons why going online will help you in school:

6. *Online research is easy and convenient.* When your parents were in school, research often meant marching to the library to look stuff up in an encyclopedia and not much more. Now we're in the early years of the Information Age. We have instant access to millions of pieces of information, pictures, graphics—and the potential to contact experts on any subject anywhere in the world. It's not that these resources weren't available before, but digital storage and retrieval means you have access to virtually any conceivable piece of information *on demand*. The Internet makes it all available to you right now, usually with just a local phone call.

5. *Online information is up-to-the-minute.* Textbook? What's a textbook? That's what students may be asking in the not too distant future. Online services and the Internet open up a world of books, newspapers, magazines, and other information sources to you with just a mouse click. And since

it's a lot easier and faster to put information on-line than to print it, information is almost always more up-to-date online than what you find in a book.

4. **It's the next best thing to being there.** Like the old song goes, ain't nothin' like the real thing, baby. But what if the real thing is halfway around the world? Most people never get the chance to go to Paris to visit the Louvre, fly to Antarctica to see penguins, or study at a university overseas. Hey, it's a big planet, and you've got homework to do. But visiting these places and thousand of other distant destinations online is the next best thing to being there. Plus it's a lot cheaper to travel virtually than to fork over the money for a plane ticket. By logging onto the Internet you can go all over the world in just seconds. Travel has always been considered an important part of education, but just think of this: One of the smartest people who ever lived was Thomas Jefferson. It took him almost two months to sail to Europe. You can get there and back "virtually" in the time it took Tom to buckle his breeches!

3. **It makes the world smaller and your mind bigger.** The same computer and modem that makes it possible for you to visit virtual museums, libraries, and other cool places all over the world also makes it possible for you to get to know people who live thousands of miles away. Want to know what life is like for kids who live in another city, state, or country? Just ask them! The online world may be the best tool ever invented for building bridges between people in different countries and cultures. "I saw the fighting in Israel on television,"

says Celeste Perri of Cold Spring Harbor High School on Long Island. "But I didn't, couldn't, know what it was like for the people who lived on both sides if I wasn't 'talking' to them every day." Plus when you're online, you can only be judged by your words and ideas—not the color of your skin, what you wear, or what you look like.

2. **It breathes new life into tired old subjects.** No matter what subject you want to talk about, someone out there is talking about it too. Science, history, literature, math—it doesn't matter what the subject is, there's a corner of cyberspace (or several corners) dedicated to it. And meeting people who are really enthusiastic about a subject you think is boring (and learning why they feel that way) could be enough to make you think twice about your least favorite subject.

And the number one reason to go online for school . . .

1. **You're going to have to learn this stuff eventually anyway, so just deal with it!** Don't be surprised if you start hearing the term "information literacy" a lot. The digital revolution means that sooner or later students and adults are going to need an entirely new set of skills: how to get information, where to find it, and how use it. Becoming a good infonaut is going to be one of the most important skills of the twenty-first century, not just in school but in the real world.

DON'T TAKE OUR WORD FOR IT . . .

Maybe the most important reason of all is that online learning is more fun than the traditional books, chalk, and notebook method. A poll conducted for *Kids Online*, a book we wrote last year, shows that most kids are already knee-deep in using the Net for school.

- Asked whether they think teaching kids how to use computers in school is important, 76 percent of kids said it is "very important," while 19 percent said it is "somewhat important."

- Seventy percent of kids said that they have used online services to research a topic for school, and fully 89 percent of respondents would rather conduct research for a school project online than "with books in a traditional library."

- When doing their homework, 84 percent of respondents said they preferred using a computer over pen and paper.

- And while they aren't exactly asking for more homework, most kids preferred increasing the online percentage in the assignment mix: 73 percent of kids surveyed said they wished their teachers would give them more projects to do online.

- On a scale of 1 to 5—with 1 being *"ugh!"* and 5 being *"wow"*—54 percent of kids rated attending school at home (through an online service) a 5, compared with 22 percent who rated it a 1.

- What academic subject would be the easiest to learn online? Kids were divided on this one: foreign language and social studies were the favorites by a slight margin (each receiving 19 percent of the vote), followed by math (16 percent), reading and writing (14 percent each), and science (11 percent).

Now keep in mind, this poll was of "wired" kids—those who are already online, so it's kind of like preaching to the converted. Most of them have already discovered how helpful it is to be online. But you get the point.

THE BOTTOM LINE

A computer and an online service can be your passport to see the world and learn. Or it can be a complete waste of time if you don't know how to find what you're looking for. This book will make sure that doesn't happen.

Getting Connected

"What helps me in school are my international pen pals. I have one in Spain. I write her in Spanish, and she writes me in Spanish. This has tremendously improved my Spanish! My other pen pals speak English, but by writing to them I learn about their cultures, which helps me understand what we're studying in world civilization class. It gives me a better perspective on the world."

—MOLLY GEBRIAN,
Conard High School
West Hartford, CT

IT'S NOT JUST FOR GEEKS ANYMORE

In the early days of the Internet, you practically needed a degree in computer science to navigate the dark corners of the digital world. Thankfully, those days are long gone. It's never been easier to take full advantage of everything there is to see and do in cyberspace.

Thousands of books have been written about choosing and buying a computer. This isn't one of them. Our guess is that you probably already have a computer and a modem, otherwise you'd be reading one of those books and not this one.

Actually, chances are pretty good that you know everything you need to know to get online. You may already have an account on America Online, Prodigy, CompuServe, or some other online service. If so, skip ahead to the next chapter. But if you're a raw beginner, then read on, newbie! In this chapter, we'll tell you what you'll need to know to get started.

HOW TO GET ONLINE

Getting online is easy, but you will need a few basic tools to get you there: a personal computer, modem, phone line, and an account with a commercial online service or an Internet access provider.

Most new computers have enough memory to handle a connection to an online service or the Internet. A modem is the first thing you need. Many computers come with built-in modems. *Modem* is short for MOdulate/DEModulate. That's geekspeak for the process that turns the bits of information streaming into your computer from the Internet into letters, numbers, pictures, and graphics you can see on your computer. You don't really need to understand how a modem works to go online, but here's something you do need to know: If you're buying a modem, get the fastest one you can afford. As commercial online services—and especially the World Wide Web—get more and more artsy with tons of graphics and pictures, a slow modem will make being online feel like pushing a cow uphill on its back.

Modems come in different baud rates—the modem's

speed—and are expressed in bps, which stands for "bits per second." Modems that run at 14.4 (that's 14,400 bits per second) are pretty much standard now. But if you're buying a modem, try to get at least a 28.8 bps modem. You'll thank us later.

A telephone line is the last piece of hardware you'll need. Modems connect you to your online service through telephone lines—the same type of line you talk on normally. You just plug your modem instead of your phone into the wall jack. If you can afford it, a second phone line dedicated to the computer is the way to go. This way you won't get hassled for tying up the phone ("there might be an emergency"—why do parents always use that excuse, anyway?). You also won't get bumped offline if someone in your house picks up an extension phone.

ONLINE VS. INTERNET

Once you've got all the hardware set up and ready, the first big decision you'll need to make is what service to use to get connected to the Internet. An online service is the door you walk through to get to all the cool stuff online. It will also give you your very own Internet e-mail address. Depending upon what you plan to do online, you might want to sign up with one of the big commercial online services or go right onto the Net through a smaller Internet access service.

You didn't know there was a difference? Some people think the Internet, AOL, CompuServe, Prodigy, and other online services are all the same thing. They're not. America Online, CompuServe, and Prodigy are "pay services." You subscribe and pay a monthly fee and hourly connection charges for a whole range of services *including* Internet access. You can use a commercial online service like AOL or Prodigy to get to nearly everything on the Internet, but it doesn't work the other way around. You can't get into the members-only areas of AOL or Prodigy from the Internet.

If you're just starting out, becoming a subscriber to one of the commercial online services is the best way to get your feet wet in cyberspace. They're easy to use and convenient (did you notice that I didn't say cheap?). All of them provide easy-to-install software, and they're well organized and monitored to make sure they're safe and kid-friendly. Commercial online services are also easier to navigate around than the Internet. Plus—and this can be very important—technical assistance is just a phone call away. All of the major commercial online services have made Internet access easily available—so you can shed the training wheels and venture out onto the Net once you're feeling comfortable in cyberspace.

HOW TO CHOOSE AN ONLINE SERVICE

The "big three" commercial online services are America Online, CompuServe, and Prodigy. All three offer the same types of services, like e-mail discussion groups, and chat areas. They have similar content—places to go for news and entertainment, for example, and areas especially for kids. So they're all the same, right? Not! Las Vegas, Nevada, and Akron, Ohio, each have a post office, several supermarkets, schools, a downtown area, and an airport, but that doesn't mean those two cities are the same. Like a city, every online service has a look and feel all its own. And choosing an online service is just like finding a city to live in—you want to find the place where you can get everything you need and where the people are friendly and you feel at home.

Let's take a quick look at each of the big three.

AMERICA ONLINE

"I was the first in my family to check out AOL, and I am the only one who knows how to get information," writes fifteen-year-old Becky Schile, a junior at Petaluma High School in California. "I explored everything on AOL until I found what I wanted. I tried using CompuServe once, but it was harder to find the information I wanted and it was not as colorful and exciting as AOL."

It's no coincidence that America Online grew from a distant third a few years ago to the eight-hundred-pound gorilla of the online world. For online beginners, it's still the best place to start. If we're turning into a country of mouse potatoes we have AOL and its more than five million members to thank. AOL practically invented point-and-click online access and left everyone else scrambling to catch up. And they haven't done it yet.

As Becky's experience demonstrates, AOL has mastered the art of convenience. People in the computer business describe it as "intuitive"—a fancy way of saying even if you've never logged onto an online service in your life, you'll be able to figure out what to do on AOL.

Installing AOL is a simple matter of loading a disk, clicking the mouse, and letting your computer do the rest. Once you're online, you'll find a "user interface" (geekspeak for what you see on the screen) that's clean, simple, and easy to use. Not only that, but it's fun to use, too. AOL also sets the standard for online communication. Its e-mail system is the best of the commercial online services, and it taught the other guys how to do live chat and instant messages.

COMPUSERVE
CompuServe was the first big commercial online service, and in many ways, it's still the leader. It's not as easy to use as AOL, and it's not designed for kids and families the way Prodigy is. But if it's information you want, you'll get it from CompuServe—by the boatload. CompuServe is like a fully loaded luxury car—hundreds of databases, newspapers, magazines, and discussion groups. But it can carry a luxury car price, since you have to pay extra for many of the best resources. On the other hand, you get access to basic services like news, sports, weather, and some basic reference tools for a flat monthly fee. CompuServe has five million members, and unlike AOL, its membership is worldwide, not just in the United States.

The New Kid on the Block—WOW! from CompuServe

CompuServe is attempting to steal America Online's thunder with its new, easy-to-use service for kids and families called WOW!. Instead of just offering an online area for kids, like the other guys, the entire service is for kids.

WOW! tries to take the confusion out of going online by being *extremely* user-friendly. There are no pulldown menus and windows, and you're never more than four mouse clicks away from anything you want to do. In addition, key functions such as Home, Help, and Quit never leave the screen, no matter where in the service you go—even when surfing the Net. It's designed to make sure you never get lost within WOW! The kids' portion of the service is divided into three basic areas: Get Smart (education), Plugged In (music, movies, computers, video games, etc.), and Play On (toys and games, sports, books, etc.).

The thing that makes WOW! such a great service for kids is its price. Unlike the other online services, you just pay one price—$17.95 a month—and you can stay online as long as you want, including surfing the World Wide Web (see Chapter Five) without putting Mom and Dad's budget in danger. Not worrying about watching the meter run while you learn your way around cyberspace is another powerful argument in favor of WOW!

A WOW! account comes with three basic paths— one for parents, one for teens, and another for younger kids. Only the parents' path has live chat and uncensored access to the World Wide Web (parents have the option of letting teens have access to live chat). The kids' path allows access to Web sites that are prescreened to make sure they contain no adult material. In addition, parents have the option of making all kids' e-mail go through their mailbox first (bet *that* starts a few arguments).

WOW! is also breaking the mold by making itself available exclusively on CD-ROM. You don't load the software onto your computer from a disk like all the other services. This gives the service an amazingly vivid, richly graphical look and feel. However, you have to own one of the powerful new multimedia Windows 95 PCs with a CD-ROM drive. A Mac platform version is planned for fall 1996. This makes the universe of potential users a lot smaller than those for the other services—a potentially risky move for WOW!

If you have the right kind of computer, another compelling reason to join WOW! is access to Infonautics' Homework Helper service (see page 34). Before WOW! came along, Homework Helper was available either on Prodigy (where you pay hourly connect charges) or for a flat monthly fee of $9.95 on the World Wide Web (in addition to the cost of your Internet access service). With its flat price of $17.95 for all services, WOW! is now the most cost-effective way to get access to Homework Helper.

In addition to Homework Helper, WOW! also offers access to On Location Education—the company that tutors child stars on the sets of Hollywood movies and TV shows. They're promising to be the Domino's Pizza of homework help—guaranteed answers to homework questions in thirty minutes (if they don't make it, will they do your homework for you?)

WOW! does have some drawbacks. When it comes to content, it doesn't have nearly as much to offer as the big three commercial online services. And the CD-ROM delivery system limits the number of potential users. But it's the most kid-friendly environment of any service. And parents will love it because of the built-in walls that can keep kids from wandering into areas of the Net that are meant for grown-ups.

☛ **HOT TIP!** As part of its plans to compete against the other commercial online services, WOW! is currently available completely free of charge to schools and teachers (even though most schools have Macs). Make sure your teacher or computer resource person at school knows!

PRODIGY

Prodigy has more than two million members in the United States, which makes it a distant third in the race among the big three, but don't let that put you off. Prodigy has always been a very kid- and family-friendly service—check out the very active Kids Zone and Teen Turf. It was also the first commercial online service to offer its members access to the Internet's World Wide Web.

Like AOL, Prodigy is a good place to get your feet wet in cyberspace. The service is a little bit slow, and basic features like e-mail, chat, and message boards can be a little confusing to use at first. But if you get lost, just click your mouse on the Member Help Center button at the top of the screen. It'll take you directly to Online Support for help.

As this book went to press, Prodigy was facing a tough time in the online business. Because of the explosion of the World Wide Web (see Chapter Five), some people were predicting the big three could turn into the big two. Stay tuned!

SUBSCRIPTION INFO

If you want to become a subscriber to America Online, CompuServe, or Prodigy you'll need special software. It's free, and finding it is no problem—you can find special membership offers and sometimes even the software in magazines like *Net Guide, Home PC, Family PC*, and *Computer Life.* Your local computer store always has supplies of free software. Or you can call the following numbers:

America Online 1-800-827-6364

CompuServe 1-800-881-8961

CompuServe/WOW! 1-800-524-3388

Prodigy 1-800-PRODIGY

☞ **EXPERT TIP!** AOL, CompuServe, and Prodigy
each cost $9.95 a month, including five free hours
of usage. However, each of the big three services
offers anywhere from five to ten free hours online
to get you to go for a test drive. Take advantage
of these offers to try them all and find out which
service is best for you!

ROAD RULES AND NETIQUETTE

If you are new to cyberspace, there are a few commonsense rules of the road you need to know. There
are also some informal rules about how to behave
online, known as "netiquette," short for "Internet
etiquette."

Following the rules of the road is important. That's
because the so-called information superhighway isn't
really a highway at all. As we've discussed, it's really
more like a city—several cities. Several big *crowded*
cities. Several big crowded cities where people buzz
around and bump into one another a lot. That means
there are bound to be people stepping on one another's toes. Or worse. People get into arguments in
the real world, often accompanied by nasty language and colorful hand gestures. And the same is
sometimes true in cyberspace. Well, maybe not the
hand gestures.

As long as people have opinions and sensitivities,
there will be disagreements. But there are a few commonly agreed upon standards of behavior online that
make it a little easier for everyone to get along to-

gether. These rules are known as netiquette. Here are a few basic dos and don'ts to remember.

Do: *Get the FAQs of life.* Many online groups, especially mailing lists and newsgroups (see Chapter Four) have a list of FAQs (frequently asked questions) for newcomers. You may find your questions have already been answered if you check there first.

Don't: *Use foul language.* Swearing in a chat room or on a message board is rude, crude, and a surefire way to lose your online account.

Do: *Lurk before you leap.* One of the fastest ways to get people annoyed with you is to barge into an online discussion or message board and ask a lot of stupid questions, no matter how sweetly and innocently you ask. Every online forum, newsgroup, or message board is like a small community where most of the people know one another. They'll almost always welcome newcomers as long as they're not pushy and aggressive. Spend a little time "lurking,"—reading and observing an online area before jumping in with your questions and comments.

Don't: *Type in ALL CAPS.* This is one of the most common newbie mistakes. Typing online with your caps lock key down is considered SHOUTING online.

Do: *Remember people's feelings.* It's sometimes easy to forget that there's a real person typing at you on your screen. If you find yourself in a disagreement with someone online, do it with courtesy and respect for their feelings.

Don't: Scroll. Scrolling is holding down the Send key in a chat room without typing a message. This makes the chat fly by so fast that it's impossible to read. This is worse than annoying. It's totally childish and immature.

Do: Be helpful. One of the things that makes being online special is what some Net vets call "virtual community." That means neighbors help neighbors. If you meet someone online who has questions and you know the answers, help him or her out. That way, they'll be more likely to help *you* when you need it. Just remember the old saying: What goes around comes around.

Don't: Be a jerk. This should be the easiest one to remember. Despite the rules of netiquette, there are too many people online who are rude, crude, dominate message boards and chat rooms, and generally make life unpleasant for everyone around them. Don't be one of them.

ONLINE SAFETY

The single most important thing to remember about being online is not to give out *any* personal information—like your full name, where you live, your phone number, etc. Your parents have always told you not to talk to strangers, and the same thing is true in cyberspace. Yes, it's a lot of fun meeting all kinds of new and different people online, but unless it's someone you know personally in the offline world—and unless you have your parents' permission—*never* give out any information that could lead strangers to your house or school.

I'm not saying you should be paranoid about on-line stalkers and creeps—you can travel far and wide in cyberspace without coming across anybody like that. But it's always better to be safe than sorry. And if someone gets you into a conversation online that makes you uncomfortable—either in a chat room or via e-mail—report them to your online service. All the commercial online services put a lot of time and effort into weeding out the weirdos, so don't be shy about speaking up!

☞ **EXPERT TIP:** Remember to keep your password a secret. Giving someone the password to your online account is like giving them the keys to your house. Try not to pick an obvious password like your first name. Make it something that only you will remember. Also, beware of scam artists who will send you messages or e-mail claiming they work for your online service and asking for your password. No one will ever ask you for your password for any reason. Don't be fooled!

The National Center for Missing and Exploited Children has a brochure called "Child Safety on the Information Highway." It suggests kids make the following online pledge:

- I will not give out personal information, such as my address, telephone number, parents' work addresses/telephone numbers, or the name and location of my school without my parents' permission.

- I will tell my parents right away if I come across any information that makes me feel uncomfortable.

- I will never agree to get together with someone I "meet" online without first checking with my parents. If my parents agree to the meeting, I will be sure that it is in a public place and bring my mother or father along.

- I will never send a person my picture or anything else without first checking with my parents.

- I will not respond to any messages that are mean or in any way make me feel uncomfortable. It is not my fault if I get a message like that. If I do, I will tell my parents right away so that they can contact the online service.

- I will talk with my parents so that we can set up rules for going online. We will decide upon the time of day that I can be online, the length of time I can be online, and appropriate areas for me to visit. I will not access other areas or break these rules without their permission.

You can get free copies of "Child Safety on the Information Highway" from the National Center for Missing and Exploited Children at 1-800-THE-LOST (1-800-843-5678). Call today and talk about it with your parents.

REALITY CHECK

OK, so now you're all excited about getting online and cruising the Net, and filling your brain with all it has to offer. So here's the bad news: Going online costs money!

Being on the celebrated info highway may be the best thing to happen to students since coed gym class, but it's not free. In fact, it can get downright expensive, if you're paying by the minute. If you don't know where to look for information, you can wind up adrift in the farthest reaches of cyberspace with the meter running. But don't worry. The whole point of this book is to turn you into a supersearcher, not a superspender.

WHO'S ONLINE?- - - - - - - - - - - - - -

Personal computers have become a permanent fixture in students' bedrooms as more kids are spending time on the computer doing homework:

- 36 percent of all American households have a computer.
- 25 percent of computer households have more than one computer.
- 89 percent of teenagers use the computer for school assignments.

—*Times Mirror;* Packard Bell Electronics, Inc.

- -

Online Reference
and Research Tools

"I was doing a report on water pollution for my school. When I was in the Kids Only section of AOL, I spotted an area called Comptons Study Break. I went into the message board and typed in that I needed info for my report. Within two days I had gotten tons of responses. One guy even e-mailed me his science fair report from last year. It really helped!"

—BARRETT THORNTON, seventh grade
the Rivers School
Wellesley, MA

LOOK IT UP!

Being smart isn't a simple matter of knowing the answers—it's knowing where to find the answers. And your computer is the great equalizer. Entire encyclopedias, dictionaries, almanacs, and scores of newspapers and magazines and hundreds of works of literature, and other reference sources are available online. You can answer almost any question with your computer. It's like they say on *The X-Files*: The truth is out there.

Your personal computer and a modem—and knowing where to look—puts it all at your fingertips. Your computer makes it possible for you to browse through the vast collections of the Library of Congress and hundreds of other online libraries, dial into cool and useful sites on the World Wide Web, hunt through countless files and databases, research in government records and files—all the tricks of the trade of the best reporters and reference librarians are now available to you! And you thought the only trick librarians knew was scrunching up their faces and going, "Sshhhhhhhh!"

The quickest and easiest way to find basic information is on one of the big commercial online services, like AOL, Prodigy, or CompuServe. Unlike the wild, untamed Internet, which we'll discuss in the next chapter, commercial online services are simple, well organized, and easy to use. As part of their basic service, they each offer research tools like encyclopedias that you can search through in the blink of an eye. For simple, everyday research questions, like "What's the capital of Nebraska?" or "Who's buried in Grant's Tomb?" they just can't be beat. The big three also offer access to online newspapers and magazines to search in for up-to-the-minute information you won't find in any textbook. In fact, that's the single best thing about getting information online instead of at the library—compared to searching in cyberspace, a textbook is as up-to-date as a tombstone!

HOW TO BE A CYBERSEARCHER

Doing research online is like being a miner. We know what you're thinking: "Just great. I'm in the dark and getting the shaft." Good one, smart guy. Yes, being a miner is hard work, but if you know where to dig and you use the right tools, you'll strike gold every time!

The specific reference and research resources are different on each of the major online services, but the types of tools they offer are basically the same. All the services provide some combination of online encyclopedia, dictionaries, magazines, and newspapers. And all of them let you do key word searches to uncover exactly the information you need.

Let's start out by looking at the biggest commercial online services—America Online, CompuServe, and Prodigy—and where to look for information on each.

AMERICA ONLINE

The main menu of AOL gives you fourteen different paths to choose. The best and most obvious is— duh!—Reference Desk. Click!

AOL's online reference desk is just like the reference desk at your local library, except there's no librarian. *You're* the librarian. The opening screen has buttons to click on for *Compton's Encyclopedia* and a dictionary. Click on the file that says General Reference, and suddenly you're looking at a whole list of reference works, including a *National Geographic* atlas with downloadable maps, a thesaurus, and something called the Macmillan Information SuperLibrary, which has lots of reference works, including one of the coolest fact books in the world, *The New York Public Library Desk Reference.*

AOL has even packaged some of their basic reference tools together for kids. Click on Especially for Kids, and you'll see a menu of offerings, including the atlas, dictionary, encyclopedia, and thesaurus—one-stop shopping! There's also a neat feature called Homework Help that will help guide you to the answers you want, either by helping you look it up in one of the reference works, letting you send an e-mail message to a teacher, or discussing it in a chat room. Check it out!

Let's take a closer look at some of the reference works on AOL.

Merriam Webster's Dictionary
(key word: MW Dictionary)

You can look up tens of thousands of words instantly in *Merriam Webster's Collegiate Dictionary*. Just type in the word and click. But you can do more than look up words. You can also learn the history of a word and when it first appeared in the English language. The kewlest thing is that unlyk a printd dikshunary, u kan yoos it efen if u'r not a grate speeler. Seriously, If you don't know how to spell the word, type in what you think may be the first few letters and an asterisk (*), then press Enter. You'll get a list of words that start with those letters to pick from. Hopefully, if you've guessed well, one will be the word you're after.

By the way, if you hit key word: "dictionary" on AOL (instead of "MW Dictionary"), you still get *The Merriam Webster's Dictionary*, but a menu pops up that lets you choose from a kids' dictionary, a medical dictionary, something called the *Dictionary of Cultural Literacy*, and *Que's Computer & Internet*

Dictionary, which lets you figure out how badly you've been flamed when someone tells you to RTFM. Or what it means when someone is LOL behind your back when you don't read the FAQ.

Compton's Living Encyclopedia and The Concise Columbia Encyclopedia
(key word: Encyclopedia)

If you've never used an online encyclopedia before, you're in for a treat. AOL offers the complete text of *Compton's Encyclopedia.* Here's where you really start to grasp the power of online research. *Compton's* consists of about ten million words in more than thirty-five thousand articles. Thumbing through that to find all the articles that contain information on the subject you're looking for might take the better part of an afternoon. But online, you can do it in a heartbeat!

Say, for example, you're doing a report on Abraham Lincoln. It would take you until your junior year in college to find every single time Lincoln is mentioned in the entire encyclopedia. But online, you can find them all in, oh, about .86 seconds. (You don't believe me? Try it yourself!) Just type in "Abraham Lincoln" and click on Search. Boom! Our sixteenth president is mentioned 174 times. *Compton's* lists them all for you and lets you read the one you want by double-clicking your mouse on the article.

Of course, not every one of those 174 entries is going to be helpful if your report is about Lincoln's Emancipation Proclamation, which ended slavery. So you can narrow the search by adding extra key words. For example, when you ask the encyclopedia to find every reference to "Lincoln and slavery," 27 article titles come up. Type in "Lincoln and Emancipation Proclamation," and you get just 7 article titles—all of which are right on target for your report.

The most important difference between a printed book and an online book is that once a book is printed and bound, it's as dead as the tree they chopped down to make the paper to print it on. So if your parents bought an encyclopedia in 1985, you're working with information that's more than a decade old. Online, a book can be updated constantly. One of the coolest features about *Compton's Encyclopedia* on AOL is a section called The Latest. Your mom and dad's 1985 encyclopedia doesn't have a single word about the baseball strike, the war in Bosnia, or last year's Nobel Prize winners. But all that and more is available in *Compton's* online encyclopedia.

The Newsstand
(key word: Newsstand)

AOL offers a good selection of nonreference works that are also useful for school. The Newsstand offers one of the best online newspapers anywhere, the *San Jose Mercury News*, along with online versions of *National Geographic, Business Week, The New York Times, The Chicago Tribune,* and ABC News, as well as a host of computer publications like *Home PC, Family PC, Windows* magazine, and *Macworld*. You can do key word searches in all of them and in many other publications to find up-to-date information for school projects.

☛ **DON'T KNOW WHERE ELSE TO TURN?** Can't find a speck of information for your report on Peruvian llama ranching anywhere, huh? Never fear. Go to the Talking About Reference message boards (key word: Reference Help). Post the information you're looking for, and AOL's Reference Desk staffers will help you figure out where to look. You can even find a live, real-time human being to help you. Stop by the Reference Desk Q & A Chat Room from 8 P.M. to midnight, Eastern time.

COMPUSERVE

CompuServe is the granddaddy of online services, and it made its reputation on its amazing depths of reference information. You name it and it's here— deep, rich databases on every imaginable subject, hundreds of newspapers and magazines, and reference works galore. If there's a problem, it's that there is too much information on CompuServe, and finding what you're looking for can be a little intimidating. Fortunately, there are a number of good, basic reference tools that are easy to use.

Grolier's Academic American Encyclopedia (GO ENCYCLOPEDIA)

The online version of the *Academic American Encyclopedia* contains the full text of the print version— over 10 million words in over 33,000 articles. It's updated four times a year, so it's always very current. A short-entry encyclopedia, *Grolier's* is perfect for finding facts for reports and projects quickly and easily. If you need more information, it offers bibliographies for more than 10,000 entries, hundreds of fact boxes and tables, and outlines for long articles. Naturally, *Grolier's* is fully searchable by key word, including cross-referencing features within articles that point out where to look for additional, relevant information.

American Heritage Dictionary
(GO DICTIONARY)

The *American Heritage Dictionary* contains over 300,000 definitions of words, phrases, famous people, and geographic locations. Searching is simple— just enter the word and hit Search. And if you don't know how to spell the word, simply type in the first five characters. *American Heritage Dictionary* will list all words matching the five characters you've entered!

Magazine Database Plus
(GO MAGDB)

Magazine Database Plus is a service that lets you retrieve full-text articles from more than 250 general-interest and niche publications. The "plus" means it's a fee service—over and above the standard CompuServe hourly charges—so use it only when you're doing research you can't do with CompuServe's encyclopedia or the *Information Please General Almanac* (GO GENALMANAC). In the many magazines on the database, you'll find articles on current events, science, sports, people, arts and education, the environment, travel, and more, in magazines as far back as 1986, many of which are updated weekly.

PRODIGY
OK, we'd better just come right out and say it: Looking for reference help on Prodigy is enough to make you a little cranky. For some unknown reason, Prodigy no longer has a separate reference area. In order to find the reference works on the service, you need to know the "jump" words for each one. This is seriously annoying.

Fortunately (maybe not) there aren't that many jump words you'll need to remember. In fact, one will do: "encyclopedia." Prodigy describes itself online as a "fact-checker's nirvana," which only shows they have a strange notion of what passes for bliss. They have the same fully searchable online version of *Compton's Encyclopedia* (jump: Encyclopedia) as AOL, but that's about it in terms of basic research tools—no dictionary, no almanac, no atlas, nothing. Well, almost nothing. They have some fun extra services, like congressional voting records, and a terrific area set up by *Consumer Reports*, but I'm not sure that quite scratches my fact-finding itch—never mind nirvana. But don't despair. The really great reference resources on Prodigy are part of an outside service called Homework Helper, which we'll discuss shortly.

The Newsstand
(jump: Newsstand)

Prodigy is a little bit light in online publications, too. They offer an online version of *Newsweek* (jump: Newsweek) in Windows format only and *Sports Illustrated for Kids* (jump: SI for kids). There's Access Atlanta (jump: Atlanta), an online version of the *Atlanta Journal-Constitution*, one of the better newspapers in the country. It's a great place to get world and national news, sports, entertainment, and more—not just news about Atlanta. Another great newspaper online is *Newsday* (jump: Newsday), which also gives you world and national news online in addition to stories about its home base of Long Island, New York. Other local papers covering Southern California, Milwaukee, Rhode Island, and Tampa are also accessible from Prodigy's newsstand.

HOMEWORK HELPER: ONE-STOP INFO SEARCHING

If Prodigy loses points for being a little thin in the reference department, they make up for it by offering access to a service that is probably the single best online resource for homework help anywhere. It's called Homework Helper, (clever, huh?) and it's available on Prodigy and the World Wide Web.

If you're an astrophysicist looking for information for your doctoral thesis on the molecular structure of gases in the atmosphere of the third moon of Uranus, then Homework Helper is not for you. But for us mere mortals, it's just about the closest thing to one-stop information shopping online as you can imagine. You name it, and it's there: encyclopedias, dictionaries, almanacs, atlases, and hundreds of maps and photos for downloading, as well as the full text of over 150 newspapers, 900 magazines, 2,000 classic books, and radio and TV transcripts out the wazoo. If your teacher asks you for information you can't find on Homework Helper, have her reported to the principal for inflicting cruel and unusual punishment.

The real breakthrough with Homework Helper is that it lets you ask a question like a normal person, not a reference librarian. Just post your question in plain English—"Do seat belt laws really save lives?"—and Homework Helper searches its entire vast collection to find the articles that best address your question.

Homework Helper has features that let you narrow or expand your search. At higher search powers, it automatically looks for many synonyms and related words and topics. On lower search power settings, it will look only for your exact words. Use the lower settings for very broad searches, and the higher power for searches about very specific questions. You can also get stuff that is appropriate to your grade level, download photos and maps (a surefire teacher pleaser), and more.

Homework Helper isn't perfect. You can't get help with math problems, for example. But it's hard to imagine a more complete and easier to use service for school. One of the biggest problems is that like too many of Prodigy's services, Homework Helper is available for Windows format only. This is frustrating for two reasons. 1. While 85 percent of the world's personal computers run Windows (Bill Gates says thank you) more than half the public schools use Macintosh computers. 2. We Mac users are $%& *@! sick and tired of being treated like second-class citizens!

Homework Helper is available on Prodigy, but you have to pay extra for it—$9.95 a month for fifty hours of use—in *addition* to your Prodigy charges. If you're not a Prodigy subscriber, however, there's good news: You can now use the World Wide Web version of Homework Helper (see Chapter Five). On the Web it goes by the name The Electric Library (http:// www.elibrary.com/) and it's a really good deal: Anyone can try the service on a free-trial basis for two weeks. After that, it's $9.95 per month for unlimited access. As you'll see a little later in the book, there are tons of free resources available to students on the Internet's World Wide Web, so it's hard to say that The Electric Library is a slam-dunk great deal. But it does put absolutely everything you could need in one place in a super, easy-to-use format. If convenience is important to you, then Homework Helper or the Electric Library is for you.

SAMPLE SEARCHES ONLINE

Now that you know your way around the commercial online services, let's go on a fact-finding mission and try a few sample searches.

> *Q: Train A leaves Los Angeles, headed east at an average speed of 75 miles an hour at 2 P.M., and train B leaves Kansas City two hours later headed west at an average speed of 60 miles an hour. If the distance between Kansas City and Los Angeles is 1,500 miles, how long will it take to fill the bathtub?*

Just kidding. Here's a real question.

> *Q: What's the tallest mountain in the world?*

Let's use Homework Helper for this one. It lets you search lots of different sources—newspapers, magazines, TV and radio transcripts, books, and more. We don't really need up-to-the-minute info for this question—mountains only change heights every billion years or so—so on the search screen, we'll ask Homework Helper to only look in Books for the answer to this question.

All we need to do is type in our question, "What's the tallest mountain in the world?," click on Search, and Homework Helper goes to work, scanning its massive database for articles that contain the words *tallest, mountain,* and *world,* (that's how it works). In a few seconds it has found 123 articles that match. The first one is listed like this:

Explorers
Score: 100; **Earth Explorer;** *;02-01-1995; Size: 12K; Reading Level: 9.*

The "100" score pretty much guarantees a direct hit on our search question. The reading level of 9 means the article is at a ninth grade reading level. When we click on the article to read it, it turns out to be a pretty long article. But here's where Homework Helper really comes in handy: At the top of the screen is a button that says Go to Best Part. Click there and you go straight to this passage:

Edmund Hillary is best known as the first man to reach the top of Mount Everest in Nepal. (Whether Hillary or his guide, Tenzing Norgay, was the actual first one at the peak is not known—and neither man would say.) At 8,848 meters (29,028 feet), Everest is the TALLEST MOUNTAIN *in the* WORLD. *Hillary was knighted for his achievement. He later wrote* High Adventure, *the story of his climb.*

Homework Helper knew to go straight to the part of the article where the words *tallest, mountain,* and *world*—all part of our question—appeared closest together. Pretty cool, huh? We got our question answered, plus learned a little about the first man to climb the tallest mountain in the world.

That was simple. Now let's try a hard one—a science question.

Q: Do mosquitoes have teeth?

Hmmm. Interesting question. They sure as heck bite, so they must chomp down with *something*. To find out what, let's go to *Compton's Encyclopedia* on AOL (key word: Encyclopedia). We'll start with a simple search for all references to mosquitoes. Click on Search All Text and type in "Mosquito" [Enter].

This turns up fifty-four mentions of *mosquito*, including articles about malaria, mosquito netting, and the Mosquito Coast. Let's see if we can narrow it a bit. By typing in "mosquito and teeth" we turn up zero articles, so that's *too* narrow. How about this: "mosquito and bite" [Enter].

Bingo! Fourteen articles including one titled "Mosquito Bites." Clicking on that article, we read the following:

> To obtain a blood meal, a female mosquito selects a likely spot on her victim and begins sawing through the skin with her mandibles and maxillae. Through her hypopharynx she injects saliva into the wound to prevent the blood from clotting so that it flows freely into her labro-hypopharyngeal tube. She then sucks up a supply of blood, stores it in her abdomen, and flies away.

Gulp. Sounds pretty gross. Close your eyes for a moment and wait for that wave of nausea to pass. There. Better? Now . . . what the heck are mandibles and maxillae? Fancy words for teeth? To find out, let's go to the dictionary (key word: Dictionary) on AOL and look those words up. Type in "mandible" [Enter].

> 1 a: JAW 1a; especially: a lower jaw consisting of a single bone or of completely fused bones; b: the lower jaw with its investing soft parts; c: either the upper or lower segment of the bill of a bird.

Nothing about teeth. Check out *maxillae* in the dictionary and —*uh-oh*—we get a scary looking message that says "No matching entries were found." A dead end? No way! Don't forget that we can approximate spellings with AOL's online dictionary. If *maxillae* is plural, and you don't know what the root word is, just type in the first few letters and an asterisk ... maxil* [Enter].

Yes! That gives us three words, including *maxilla*:

1 a: JAW. 2: one of the first or second pair of mouthparts posterior to the mandibles in insects, myriapods, crustaceans, and closely related arthropods.

Whatever. The important part is that mosquitoes may bite, but they're all jaws. Our search is over. Do they have teeth? The answer is no.

☞ **EXPERT TIP:** When you're looking up long articles in an online encyclopedia, newspaper, or magazine, stopping to read each article takes time and will run up your online bill. If you're paying hourly connect charges to be online, get in the habit of saving the articles you've searched for onto your computer's hard drive and then logging off and reading them offline.

PLAN YOUR SEARCH AND SEARCH YOUR PLAN

There is no right or wrong way to look for information online. The only rule is "whatever works, works." Still, make sure you don't waste time if you're paying by the minute to be online. Before you go online to look for information, give some thought to where you're likely to find it—the online encyclopedia? Newspapers and magazines? Which one? Look for *information* online, not ideas. If you know what you want and have some ideas where to start looking, your search will be quick and easy!

The most important thing about online research is to focus. Being a supersearcher means knowing what you're looking for and finding the straightest route to your destination. Avoid being tempted by off-the-wall subjects and eye-catching graphics that have absolutely nothing to do with the reason you logged on in the first place.

THE NEXT STEP

Being online is a great way to interact, not just with information, but people. A little later, we'll talk about how to use message boards, e-mail, and other tricks to find everything from experts on dozens of subjects to live online teachers to help you with your homework.

Now that you've mastered the basics of using commercial online services for research, you're ready to take the next giant leap—out onto the Internet.

Searching the Internet

"The e-mail that I send and receive from eleven different countries across the globe has given me a greater appreciation of the size of the world, the cultural differences (language, etc.), but it has also shown me how we are so much the same!"

—BRANDON BRUCE, senior
Cate School
Carpinteria, CA

Now that you've learned your way around the big commercial online services and learned the basics of searching for information, you're ready to venture beyond the brightly lit corridors of AOL, Prodigy, and CompuServe and venture out into the wild, untamed Internet.

The Internet is an exciting, fast-growing phenomenon. It's a mountain of information that dwarfs what's available on the commercial online services. That's the good news. The bad news is that it can be a confusing and frustrating place to try to find your way around. This chapter is your guide to what's out there and how to find it. We'll explore how to use basic Internet tools, like e-mail, newsgroups, and Gopher, to find information online.

WHAT IS THE INTERNET?

The Internet is not just a big online service like AOL, Prodigy, CompuServe, or WOW! The Internet is not a computer network. It's a network of networks—an almost unimaginably huge collection of computers at colleges; businesses; local, state, and federal government offices; museums and libraries; individual homes—and more than a few garages—all seamlessly connected to one another by computer cables and phone lines.

INTERNET TOOLS

Think of the Internet as the biggest, busiest city in the world. Millions of people have access to the Internet—at least thirty million in over one hundred countries around the world. And as soon as you have an e-mail address, you are connected to every one of them. You'll also have some powerful ways to use your computer to burrow for information in other computers across the globe.

Let's look at some basic Internet tools.

E-MAIL
The most popular and simple Internet tool is electronic mail, or e-mail for short. In many ways, it's also the most powerful part of the Internet. E-mail can be a simple but effective way to bring reports and projects to life. If your assignment is to learn more about Ireland, for example, what better way than to write to people who live there and ask them

questions? You can also use e-mail to interview experts in whatever subject you're working on for school. Or you can use it to work on projects with other kids.

If you have an online account, you have an e-mail address. Your screen name or user ID is your e-mail address. It's that simple. Once you have an account with AOL, Prodigy, CompuServe—or almost any other online or Internet access service—you've got everything you need to receive and send electronic messages all over the world.

E-mail is universal. In other words, if you have an AOL e-mail address, you can write to people who are on other online services. My e-mail address is RPondiscio@aol.com. The first part of that address, RPondiscio is my AOL user name. The @ symbol is how you know you have a valid Internet e-mail address. The third part of the address is called the domain. In this case, the domain is America Online, which is a *commercial* service—hence "aol.com." If you're on AOL, you don't need to include the "@aol.com" part of the address to write to me. If you're on a different service, the computer uses the "@aol.com" information to route your message to my mailbox. Drop me a line! I always write back.

E-mail addresses can also tell you a little about who you're writing to. If the address ends in ".edu," that means the address is part of an educational computer system, like the ones found at most colleges or your school—so the person you're writing to is probably a student or teacher. There are others: ".org" means the address is a nonprofit organization; ".mil" means it's a military address; ".gov" means government address; ".com" is a commercial service like

AOL, Prodigy, or CompuServe, or a business. Every for-profit organization is ".com."

It doesn't matter if you're sending e-mail from a .com address to a .edu address. And it doesn't matter whether you're writing e-mail on a Mac and sending to someone with a PC running Windows. E-mail uses something called a standard protocol. Standard protocol simply means that any computer wired to the Net can send e-mail to any other computer wired to the Net.

E-mail is the most commonly used online tool, and for good reason. It's easier than typing and faxing, and it usually arrives at its destination in seconds—even halfway around the world. Plus, the electronic post office is open twenty-four hours a day, seven days a week! Lots of kids take advantage of the speed and convenience of e-mail to write every day to "key pals" (the online version of pen pals) all over the world—for school *and* for fun!

For example, students in Mrs. Beth Lowrey's fourth grade class in Athens, Georgia, practice their writing skills and learn social studies with key pals in Canada, Australia, and England. At the Abington Friends School in Jenkintown, Pennsylvania, students in every grade have e-mail pals. Technology coordinator Lynne Mass helps kids find key pals from all over the world on the Internet.

"For my last three years at Cold Spring Harbor High School, I was the coeditor of an international literary magazine called *A Vision*," says Celeste Perri, who is now a college freshman. "Most of the work was done through simple e-mail and, in the case of the artwork and photography, snail mail.

"What made the experience beautiful was the people," Celeste recalls. "My high school is in a small town on the north shore of Long Island. Probably I never would have met students in mainland China, students in Ramallah, students in Siberia if it were not for this project. And the people I was working with were people just like me—they were students with their whole futures ahead of them. We weren't even talking politics most of the time. We were telling each of the stories we had, the stories that tie us together as humans."

FINDING KEY PALS ON THE NET-- -- -- -- -- --

"I got a Spanish pen pal through an organization called Earth Friends," says Molly Gebrian, who goes to Conard High School in West Hartford, Connecticut. "I'm now a rep for them and find other kids who want international pen pals. They can have them through the Net or the postal mail. Most of mine are key pals, but I have a few who aren't. I love writing to them and learning about their cultures!"

How many kids have you met from other countries? Molly's made friends online in Spain, Belgium, Germany, the Ukraine, South Africa, Singapore, Australia, New Zealand, and Iceland. You can find Earth Friends by writing to EarthFrnds@aol.com. Tell them Molly sent you!

You can find a cool key pal almost anywhere online. Look in places on your online service set up just for kids or in areas about subjects you're interested in like movies, sports, or music. If you're having trouble finding a key pal, here are some suggestions:

• You can meet other kids at Kids Only Online (key word: KOOL) and the Global Links bulletin board of the Electronic Schoolhouse (key word: ESH). Edmark Corporation (key word(s): Edmark, penpal), an educational software company, also runs a bulletin board on AOL for kids to find key pals.

- On Prodigy, the best place to meet a key pal is in the Teens bulletin board (jump: teens bb). Post a note telling about yourself and the type of key pal you're looking for. There's also a Girls Only bulletin board (jump: teen girlz ltd), where the girls can go to dish on the guys. CompuServe kids can find key pals in the Students' Forum (GO STUFO).

On the World Wide Web, a number of services are popping up to set kids up with online friends to exchange e-mail with. Here are three good ones:

Find a Keypal
(http://www.kidscom.com/keypal.html)
Internet for Kids, Inc.
(http://www.internet-for-kids.com/)
The Pen-pal Box
(http://plaza.interport.net:80/kids_space/mail/pen/pen.html)

Don't be confused by these web addresses. I'll explain how they work in the next chapter!

MAILING LISTS
Mailing lists or "ListServs," have been around since the dawn of the Internet. And they're still one of its most popular features. That's because almost everyone can participate in an Internet mailing list. You

don't need expensive software or fancy browsers—just plain vanilla e-mail!

When you hear the term "mailing list," you might think of the things companies use to send you information about stuff you don't really need. You're probably thinking, "mailing list? Is that like junk mail?" Not at all. Mailing lists are Internet discussion groups on all kinds of subjects—everything from Brazilian rain forests to Beavis and Butthead. They let people keep in touch and up to date on the latest news about all kinds of things that are important to them.

One of the coolest things about the Internet, for example, is finding out that even though you might be the only person in East Clintwood, New Jersey, who owns a pet iguana, there is an Internet mailing list all about them online with dozens of other people who are just as crazy about iguanas as you are. Or maybe they're just as crazy as you. Whatever. When you subscribe to a mailing list, you can participate in two ways: You can send an e-mail message, or "post," to everyone on the list, or you can send private e-mail to individual members. It's a great way to make online friends who share your interests!

Nobody knows how many mailing lists exist on the Internet, although directories of mailing lists can be found in lots of places: On AOL, go to the Internet Connection (key word: Internet) and click on Mailing Lists to search for topics of interest to you. Or point your web browser (see Chapter Five) to http://www.liszt.com/.

A word of warning: Mailing lists can be highly technical, very advanced information about *unbelievably* narrow topics. You might not get too much out of the burning physics issues being discussed in the

Time Domain Reflectometry Discussion List, for example. If it's just basic information you need, mailing lists probably won't be your first choice of Internet research tools. On the other hand, if you really want to know a lot about a subject and mix it up with real experts, mailing lists are good places to find them. But in general, it's best not to subscribe to an Internet mailing list unless you are *really* passionate about the subject being discussed, since some lists can fill your online mailbox faster than water fills a sinking ship. And once you subscribe to a mailing list, remember your netiquette! Mailing lists are often like private clubs where newcomers must work hard to prove themselves to the old-timers.

NEWSGROUPS

Newsgroups, also known as Usenet newsgroups, are another popular feature from the early days of the Internet. Like mailing lists, they are terrific places to learn a lot about a specific subject from people who really know their stuff. Unlike mailing lists, all the conversation is stored on an online bulletin board, instead of delivered to your mailbox.

There are thousands upon thousands of newsgroups devoted to every imaginable subject—you name it, it's there. One of the greatest things about newsgroups is that, when you join, you actually feel as though you're part of a special club or cool hangout—and you are! Although all newsgroups are devoted to single subjects, people find all kinds of ways to talk about related interests. You can post messages to ongoing conversations and respond to others' opinions. You can start a new topic, or "thread," of your own. Or you can pick up the conversation on a thread that no one has responded to in a while and rekindle discussion. Just as in real life, however, conversations can get pretty heated—especially when the conversation turns to sensitive issues. People sometimes get hot under the collar, rant, rave, and can become, well, verbally abusive. In netspeak, this type of behavior is called flaming. Our advice—stay clear of hotheads and always remember your netiquette.

If you are interested in a topic, but don't want to get mail about it nearly every day, newsgroups might be for you. On a mailing list, you have to read every single message. In a newsgroup, however, you can come and go as you please. You can skip all the messages that aren't interesting or important to you.

GOPHER

Gopher is an Internet tool—a friendly little rodent who will "go-fer" information all over the Internet and bring it home to you. Strangely enough, that's not why it's called Gopher. The Golden Gopher is the mascot of the University of Minnesota, the university where this search tool was invented. Just be glad it wasn't invented at the University of California— Santa Cruz, which has the banana slug for a mascot. Can you imagine how long it would take to search every corner of the Internet with a banana slug? Go Slugs!

With Gopher, just type in a key word for the information you want—*computers* or *music*, for example— and Gopher will give you a list of gopher sites to search for more information, such as catalogues, databases, software, and files. Unlike the graphics-heavy World Wide Web, which we'll discuss in the next chapter, Gopher sites are almost all just text— simple lists of menu items that point you to the information you're looking for.

America Online lets you conduct Gopher searches from the Internet Connection (key word: Internet). CompuServe and Prodigy let you access Gopher and FTP sites (see below) on the World Wide Web, which makes searches a breeze!

FILE-TRANSFER PROTOCOL (FTP)

As you might guess from the name, file-transfer protocol is the system that allows you to transfer text files, graphics, and software and download them from other computers to yours.

Until the World Wide Web arrived on the scene, FTP accounted for more traffic on the Internet than any other service. It can still be useful for downloading a piece of software from a faraway Internet site; however, you'll probably find all the software you could ever want or need to download in the software libraries of your commercial online service, especially CompuServe and AOL.

If things like Gopher and FTP sound confusing, don't worry. Many computer users can spend half their lives online and never use any of the older Internet tools. That's because of the revolution that's occurring on the Internet with the growth of the World Wide Web.

5

The World Wide Web

"Through the Internet, I now know people from around the world, all of whom are just as concerned about the world's problems as I am. I know boys and girls in Italy, England, Israel, Japan, and Germany. We are getting a head start on solving tomorrow's problems. We can actually help make the world a better place, which I think is pretty incredible."

—SHEILA KUMAR, 13
Los Angeles, CA
a delegate to the 1995 Global
Information Infrastructure
Junior Summit in Tokyo

SURFING THE PLANET

The Internet's World Wide Web (WWW) is the hottest and fasting growing frontier in cyberspace. It's growing like a weed with millions of home pages available online and thousands more sprouting up every week! The Web is a wide-open global network perfect for kids on the prowl for information and fun.

The good news is that the Web explosion has

prompted all the major commercial online services like AOL and CompuServe to open a gateway, meaning you can get access to the Web no matter which online service you're a member of. The bad news is that *getting* there is the easy part. Unlike AOL or Prodigy, no one owns the Web, so it can be a confusing place. It's difficult and frustrating to find your way around without a road map. No, make that *impossible* to find your way around without a road map. In this chapter we'll take the mystery out of the Web, explain how to use Web browsers to find your way around, and how to search for information by subjects and key words with search engines you can use for free.

A BRIEF HISTORY OF THE WEB

The Web is the multimedia component of the Internet. Think of it this way: If the Internet is like a regular desktop computer, the Web is a multimedia machine that comes with tons of CD-ROM programs that offer cool paint-and-click screens, pictures, sound, and video. The World Wide Web caused the huge explosion in the Internet's popularity by making the Internet easier to use than ever before.

Although the Internet has been around in one form or another for about twenty-five years, the World Wide Web is a fairly recent innovation. It began in 1990 at a physics laboratory in Switzerland. Many inventions end up being used for completely different things than their inventors intended, and the Web is no exception. The scientists who invented the Web built it so they could share documents and data with other physicists all over the world.

That's still a perfectly valid use of the Web. But it

has grown far beyond the wildest imaginings of its creators to become a massive global information flea market, visited by millions of people. Like a flea market, it can be confusing and chaotic. But sometimes you can stumble upon something that's just perfect for you.

In the last chapter, we talked about Gopher, FTP, and other Internet tools. Using many of these tools can be a little complicated, and as the Internet grew, the need to use all of those different tools to access different documents got confusing. That's why the Web was invented. It makes all the different kinds of documents on the Internet universally readable.

Most important, the Web has forever changed the way online information is presented. Something called hypertext markup language (HTML) creates links from one page to another. When you look at a home page, you'll notice some words look different—they may be in a different color or highlighted. These words are hypertext links. When you move your mouse over a hypertext link, the cursor arrow turns into a finger. This means you can point at the word, click your mouse, and jump to another page that has something to do with that word. This makes it incredibly easy to find information online. You can move effortlessly from one page to another to get where the information you need is stored. It's totally seamless! That's why people say they're "surfing" the Web—just like channel surfing on TV, you keep on clicking until you find what you're after or something cool and interesting!

You might be reading a document about the solar system, for example, and see the word *Jupiter* highlighted in a bright color or underlined. That indicates that it's a hypertext word. Click your mouse on the highlighted word and you'll go straight to a different document about Jupiter. These links let you move quickly and easily from one page to the next, even from one Web site to a completely different one! This interconnected linking gives the Web its name.

But it's not just hypertext that makes it so cool. The Web also brought multimedia to the Internet. Later on, we'll talk about Web browsers, a type of software that makes it possible to see graphics, photos, moving pictures, and sound on the Internet, all of which can be viewed or played with a simple mouse click.

SEARCHING THE WEB

What makes the Web so much fun and so popular is that it is really easy to use. For years you had to be a serious computer geek to navigate around the "real" Internet. With the World Wide Web, it's all point and click.

And there's plenty to point and click your way around:

- Students at Woodland High School in California go on the Web for lots of different classes—downloading up-to-date weather maps for science class, visiting sites about Native Americans for social studies, and visiting the Web Museum in Paris for the art class.

- Kids who are connected to the Web 66 site—a network of schools on the Web—work together to share information on school projects, learning about life in other states and countries.

- Students at an elementary school in Turlock, California, have had live chats on the web with dozens of famous people, including one exciting exchange with the #1 best-selling children's author, R. L. Stine—which led to two kids in the class becoming main characters in one of his books!

The Web is an interconnected series of colorful screen displays called home pages. These pages range from vast treasure troves of useful information to totally mindless wastes of time. The Web is a dream for research, because the best home pages on a subject are almost always linked to lots of other pages on the same subject. This can make your online detective work fun and exciting as you narrow in on your target. If you're on the trail of a particular piece of information and the home page you're looking at doesn't have it, you can probably track down the information by simply following your nose, clicking on one hypertext link after another until you find what you want.

GETTING STARTED: WHAT'S A URL?

At the end of a lot of ads in newspapers and magazines, and on TV—even on the sides of buses—you might notice a string of what looks like meaningless letters and symbols that look like this:

http://www.goofball.com

Gibberish? A misprint? The columnist Dave Barry jokes that those strings of letters are instructions to Dan Rather from his home planet. What's the frequency, Kenneth? Actually, it's a World Wide Web address, called a URL (it rhymes with hurl), or uniform resource locator.

The URL is the Web equivalent of a phone number. If you know someone's phone number, you can reach him at any time by picking up the phone and dialing. If you know the URL of a particular Web site, you can go there any time by typing the URL into your Web browser.

Let's take apart a URL and see how it works. When coauthor Robert Pondiscio is not on the Net, he works for *Time* magazine. Here's *Time*'s URL on the Web:

http://www.pathfinder.com/time/.welcome.html

The first part of the URL is called the protocol. The protocol is always followed by a colon and two slashes. The "http" stands for hypertext transfer protocol, which is the most common type of Web protocol.

The second part of the URL is the domain. The domain tells you who has what you're after. In this case, the domain is Pathfinder, which is TimeWarner's Web site. Pathfinder is a commercial service—that's what the ".com" means.

The third part of the address is called the path name. Your computer has subdirectories (if you've got a PC) or folders (if you have a Mac) to organize different kinds of software and files. Likewise, every domain on the Web has subdirectories or folders called path names. In this case, the URL is telling the Pathfinder domain that it wants to access *Time* magazine's path; it does so by specifying /time/. The "welcome.html" is *Time* magazine's home page.

When you think about it, a URL is not that much different from the address of your house. If you were giving directions to someone from far away, you'd have to tell her how to get to your state, then your town, then to your house. The URL is giving your computer directions to the information you want, using protocol, domain, and pathname.

☛ **VERY IMPORTANT!** URLs have to be typed in *exactly* right or they will not work. This is a royal pain in the butt, because, make the slightest little mistake—make an uppercase letter lowercase, confuse a hypen (-) with an underscore (_)—and you're toast. And some URLs are as long as both your arms! Someday, getting to a Web site will be as easy as tuning a channel on a TV set, but we're not there yet. Hey, we told you this is the *dawn* of the Information Age!

WEB BROWSERS

Now that we've got the basics out of the way, let's surf!

In order to venture out onto the World Wide Web, you need something we mentioned earlier called a Web browser, a kind of software that allows you to see the information stored at a Web site with pictures, graphics, and sound, instead of just words. Commercial online services, like AOL, Prodigy, and CompuServe, now offer their own Web browsers, which you can download for free and use to venture outside the walls built around the services and go out onto the Web.

Mosaic was the first Web browser. It was invented by a then twenty-four-year-old student named Marc Andreesen. He got a job at school (University of Illinois) to write a program that would let scientists look at 3-D models. But Andreesen was a super cybergeek who wanted to write a program that would let him navigate the Internet more easily—and also let him look at cool graphics—so he ended up writing Mosaic! Today, he helps run Netscape Communications, which makes state-of-the-art Web browsers. And he makes more money than Deion Sanders and Madonna combined. See, sometimes it really *is* worth it to do extracredit work!

America Online and Prodigy use their own exclusive browsers. Prodigy's is easy to use and lets you see all the cool, new features of the Web, such as tables, frames, and Java apps (see "The Next Wave on the Web," page 76). AOL's is still a few steps behind. CompuServe uses Spyglass Mosaic (see page 60).

You don't *have* to use the browser provided by your online service. There are others available. If you are using a direct-access Internet service, you will need a separate Web browser. They're easy to get and easy to use—just visit one of the Web sites listed below and download a trial copy of one of these Web browsers. You might even find you like some of these browsers better than the ones available through your online service. A word to the Web-wise: Don't use a text-only browser if you can possibly help it. The Web is so rich in color, sound, pictures, and video that you'd be missing most of what it has to offer by surfing in black and white.

Let's look at some of the most popular Web browsers.

NETSCAPE NAVIGATOR
Mosaic may have been the first Web browser, but it was quickly leapfrogged by Netscape Navigator, which is the browser of choice for three out of every four people on the Web.

Netscape Communications corp. (http://home.net
scape.com) makes Netscape Navigator 2.0, the newest
version. It's easy to use, and it lets you see a lot of
neat multimedia applications (like simple animation,
sound, and video), frames (windows that divide a
screen into parts so that one area remains frozen
while you scroll through the content of another),
blinking text, and more.

Netscape Navigator is easy to download and set
up, but you've got to have a direct Internet connection (not a commercial online service) to use the latest version. It was originally given away on the
Internet. Today, the company charges $49 for the lat-
est version of the browser; however, you can still
download it for free and take it for a thirty-day test
drive before you pay for it.

Netscape Navigator comes with an e-mail application that lets you send Web documents, along with
regular e-mail. Graphics load *much* faster than previous versions and faster in general than with most
other browsers. It's easy to bookmark your favorite
places on the Web; Navigator also automatically
checks to see which of your favorite places have
changed since the last time you visited them.

"Netscape is a blessing in reducing the learning
curve in order to be an effective user of the net," says
Armand Jaques, who just retired after thirty years as
a teacher at Woodland High School in Woodland,
California. "Students become effective users in about
five minutes."

MICROSOFT INTERNET EXPLORER
Attention, users of PCs and Windows 95: Microsoft
Internet Explorer 2.0 is your browser. Available from
Microsoft Corp. (http://www.microsoft.com), it's very,

very easy to use, you can launch it right from Windows 95 (no more monkeying around with Winsocks!); and has eye-popping 3-D and multimedia effects built in. All that, and it's free!

You can store Web site addresses right on your desktop by dragging them from the browser. Then, whenever you want to go to the site, just double-click from your desktop. In other words, you don't always have to keep the browser open—you can quickly activate it to go to a specific place whenever you want by just clicking on the site.

You don't have to go to a completely separate site to download video players to look at .AVI video clips; Windows 95 and explorer work together to configure a player for you on the spot from your computer.

SPYGLASS MOSAIC
You can go to the Spyglass, Inc. site (http://www. spyglass.com) to download a copy of Spyglass Mosaic, version 2.1, for a thirty-day trial, but if you want a permanent copy, you'll have to get it from CompuServe, which uses Spyglass Mosaic as its main browser.

Although it's easy to navigate the Web with Spyglass Mosaic's new and improved controls—and the graphics download pretty quickly—the browser still can't support frames, blinking text, or many multimedia features. Spyglass Mosaic offers access to e-mail, FTP, Gopher, and Usenet newsgroups.

NCSA MOSIAC
It might not have all the bells and whistles of the other three major browsers, but NCSA Mosaic 2.0 (http://www.ncsa.uiuc.edu) works just fine, thanks,

and it's very user-friendly. You do need a PC running Windows to use it, though. Its toolbar features easy-to-understand icons and tool tips; it even offers you a few hot lists to get you started, and you can add new ones easily.

The new Autosurf feature will store any number of a Web site's HTML links that you want in the browser itself. This means that you can look at a whole Web site without having to be connected to the Web, because Autosurf has saved them all in its memory! This is a really handy feature if you're paying hourly connect-time charges and your parents get edgy about high online bills (and don't they all?) Just Autosurf to a site, disconnect, and surf it charge free offline!

☛ **HOT TIP!** It's sometimes easy to get lost on the Web. You can jump in at any point and wander from site to site in any order. Even worse, you can get distracted easily (at least we do) and forget where you saw the good stuff you wanted to save. Use your Web browser to make a bookmark of pages with valuable information as soon as you see them. Then you can easily go back by choosing the site from your bookmark menu—the cyberspace equivalent of leaving behind a trail of bread crumbs. When you're working on a project for school, you might find it helpful to save bookmarks for all the important sites you come across until you're done with the assignment.

START YOUR SEARCH ENGINES!

Having a Web browser enables you to navigate the Web. But you still need to know where to navigate to. Some Web browsers come with built-in links to powerful tools for searching the Web or a Web directory, which makes it fairly simple to find what you're looking for quickly and easily. These tools are called search engines, and there are lots of good ones to help you find exactly what you want.

Just like the card catalogue at your local library, search engines can save you lots of time if you bring a little know-how to the process. You can search for a subject (type in "math" or "computer programming"), the name of a specific site ("Sports Illustrated for Kids"), a person ("Bill Clinton")—any key word that gives the search engine an idea of what you're after. Then the engine will return with a list of Web sites, complete with hypertext links, that match your key word.

There are dozens of search engines on the Web. Here are some of the biggest and best.

YAHOO (http://www.yahoo.com)

Yahoo, the granddaddy of search engines, is the most popular search engine on the Web. If you want to find *everything* on the Web on a certain topic, Yahoo will deliver. It will search its entire database of millions of Web pages and list everything that matches, twenty-five sites at a time.

It's easy to use, well organized, and flexible. Yahoo's home page has an index of all the major categories you might want to search—from entertainment to news to science to computers, and lots more—and these categories are broken down further, so you can target your search more specifically. Or you can search all over the Web quickly and easily simply by typing in a key word.

With Yahoo, search results are often *too* broad.

They include every site that mentions your key word. Say, for example, you're doing a report about France. If you enter "France" as a key word and ask Yahoo to search for every Web site where France is mentioned as a subject, it turns up 328 sites—everything from French movies to the Tour de France bicycle race. You could spend an awful lot of time looking through each listing trying to find general information for your report. Plus there is no guarantee that these sites have *good* information—they could have been created by someone who knows as little about France as you do! (See "Seeing Is Not Believing," page 70.)

Yahoo provides links to other search engines, in case you haven't found what you're looking for. For example, if you click on the Lycos hotlink after getting the results of your Yahoo search on France, you go straight to the Lycos search engine—and it automatically begins searching for additional Web sites about France.

LYCOS (http://www.lycos.com)
For raw Web searching power, Lycos may be the king of search engines. It claims to track 91 percent of the Web which, if true, is a mind-boggling percentage. You pretty much have to take their word for it, however, since no one knows for sure just how many Web pages are out there. After you type in a search or query, Lycos checks its catalogue and displays a sorted list of hits. The list is sorted in order of relevance to your query. Among items with the same relevance, the most popular sites are listed first.

Lycos uses computer programs called spiders to constantly scan the Internet, automatically keeping track of new Web pages that appear. In fact, the name *Lycos* comes from the Latin word for wolf spider. Lycos adds, deletes, and updates about fifty thousand documents a day in its catalog, so the Lycos catalog is never outdated. Lycos is easy to use and has a very intuitive interface, which means you can pretty much figure out how to use it just by looking at it.

Lycos's Web Reviews section rates sites on a 1 to 50 scale in terms of content, experience, and presentation. It's divided by section, including Education, Entertainment, and Kids, so you can find the best site for your search—or just surf! Lycos also offers the Lycos 250—a hot list of 250 sites based not on its own judgment but on how many hits these sites get. The Lycos 250 is also divided into categories: Business, Education, Entertainment, Reference, Government, News, Sports, Travel, Weather, and Web Resources.

MAGELLAN (http://www.mckinley.com)

Unlike Yahoo and Lycos, Magellan only searches Web sites that its staff has reviewed. The user interface is extremely easy and friendly, and there are lots of search options. For example, you can request that the results of your search be displayed between ten and fifty sites at a time; you can request short, medium, or long descriptions of each site; and a minimum rating—Magellan rates each site's excellence on a scale of one to four stars, with four as the best possible score.

Yahoo and Lycos are terrific search engines if you want quantity. For quality, try Magellan. As we've mentioned, it's hard to know whether a Web site is worth visiting or a complete waste of time unless you've been there and checked it out. Magellan's staff has been there and has checked out thousands of sites. That means that though you won't get as many hits on your Magellan search as you will with Yahoo or Lycos, the hits you do get will be worth visiting. Parents (or kids) can even narrow searches to include only green light sites—those sites that contain no content for "mature audiences."

Like other search engines, Magellan works with key words. Just enter one or more words in the Search box and click on Search Magellan. It doesn't matter whether you use capital or lowercase letters. If you enter more than one word, Magellan will automatically find pages that contain one or more of them. For example, if you enter "American history," Magellan directs you to sites that contain either *American* or *history* or both. It then ranks sites according to relevancy—that is, the number of times those words appear and how close together they are. The more relevant the site, the higher it goes on the list.

MORE WEB SEARCH ENGINES

ALTA VISTA (http://www.altavista.digital.com/)

Digital Equipment Corporation's Alta Vista searches billions of words on nearly twenty million Web pages. Alta Vista also searches Usenet newsgroups. You can also request advanced searches using special query language. Alta Vista's hardware and software is very impressive, but doing a search here is kind of like casting your net into the middle of the Pacific Ocean—you get a *lot* of stuff fast, but you might spend a lot more time sorting the good picks from the bad.

EXCITE (http://www.excite.com)

Excite's claim to fame is that it searches for concepts, not just key words. Usually, when a search engine looks for a site, it reports any site that even mentions your key word; that's why you sometimes end up with so many sites that have nothing to do with what you're looking for. Excite, however, searches on themes or concepts, which means that it will usually pull up the most relevant sites to your search. Excite does have a Net directory with reviews of sites, arranged by category, but it only holds fifty thousand sites.

OPEN TEST INDEX (http://www.opentext.com/)

Open Text searches every word of every Web Page the company has indexed—that's over twenty-one billion words and phrases in all. If that's more than you need (and it probably is), focus your search by searching only titles or links.

POINT (http://www.pointcom.com/)

Sometimes when you're surfing the Web, you'll come across a really great site that has a starburst logo on it that reads "Top five percent of the Web." That's Point's seal of approval, and it almost always means the site is one of the best of its kind. If you're looking for general information on a subject, you can save yourself a lot of time by limiting your searches to just these sites using Point's search engine.

WEBCRAWLER (http://www.webcrawler.com)

WebCrawler, which is owned and operated by America Online, is another good, basic search engine but not as comprehensive as the others.

WHO?WHERE? (http://www.whowhere.com)

This is basically an Internet White Pages. Just type in the name of the people whose e-mail addresses you're looking for—and where they work or go to school, if you know—and if it's out there, Who?Where? will find 'em! It will even correct misspelled names. At least in theory. It's still a work in progress, which is a polite way of saying it's not very complete. We tried to find a few of our wired friends to no avail—heck, we even tried to find ourselves! We were, however, able to track down MTV VJ-turned-Internet-consultant Adam Curry and Microsoft fearless leader Bill Gates. Our conclusion is that Who?Where? is a useful search engine for finding fairly famous folk on whom you're writing a report—or who might be able to provide useful information via e-mail.

☛ **HOT TIP:** Add search engines to your bookmark list. Every Web browser comes with a bookmark or hot link feature that will automatically save the URLs of your favorite Web sites. When you bookmark a site, you are simply telling your browser to keep a record of the URL of the site. So next time you want to visit, you just click on your bookmark, instead of typing in http://blahblahblah.com. Cool, huh? This will save you lots of time when you're looking up information on the Web!

SAMPLE SEARCHES ON THE WEB

Now that we've mastered the basics and got the lingo down, let's try a couple of real searches for information you might use for a school paper, report, or project.

ASSIGNMENT: Write a report about a foreign country

What do you know about Australia besides its a country down under where kangaroos and koala bears live? Not much, huh? No problem. If the assignment is to learn about another country, we're just a few mouse clicks away from everything you could want or need to know—history, major industries, geography, whatever.

If you don't have a specific URL of an Australia site, it's easiest to start with one of the search engines we discussed earlier.

Start by going to Yahoo (http://www.yahoo.com). On the opening screen, you'll see fourteen categories of information listed alphabetically. Arts, Business, Computers . . . all the way down to Regional. Under Regional, click on Countries. That takes us to an alphabetical list of countries, with Australia, naturally, pretty close to the top. You'll notice a number in parentheses right next to the hypertext link for Australia—that's the number of Web sites indexed by Yahoo that mention Australia—over a thousand in all! Click on Australia, and the list gets broken down further. The options include business, cities, and education—nothing that sounds like what we need for our report. So at this point let's do a search. Searching only the Web sites about Australia (Yahoo offers this option), enter in "Australia, history, info." This means we're telling the search engine we want sites that contain information about Australia *and* history *and* general information. Hit Return and four sites are listed including one for the Australian embassy in Washington, which includes "information on Australian tourism, trade, immigration, visas, geography, history, weather, and much more." We're home free!

When you think about it, the Australian embassy is a logical place to turn to for information about Australia. But we didn't think of it when we began our search. Who even knew they had a Web site? That's the beauty of search engines. They find stuff you never knew was there!

Remember, we're not saying this is the "right" way to find out information on this subject. There are lots of search engines, lots of Web sites, and many different routes to your destination—and many different destinations! The great thing about the Web is that there's practically no limit to the number of routes you can take to find out the answer to any question, and there's almost always dozens—even hundreds—of different places to find the information you're after. Like they say in car commercials, "your mileage may vary."

Let's try another one!

ASSIGNMENT: What is global warming? How is it caused?

The environment is one of the most popular topics on the Internet. There must be hundreds of Web sites about global warming, but where are they? If you don't know, it's back to Yahoo or another search engine, such as Magellan. The fourteen categories on the opening screen don't include environment, but there is a subject heading for science. Click there and a list of specific science topics comes up. There are over one thousand Web sites in the Earth Science list alone! Click on it and it gets broken down yet again, into sites about floods, hurricanes, tornadoes, daily weather news, and more. Nothing about global warming, so it's time to search. Type in "global warming" and hit Return, and once again Yahoo comes through like a champ, giving us a list of six Web sites, including one called world climate report, which says it offers "the latest news relating to global warming, or cooling, and global climate changes. Everything we need should be there!

SEEING IS NOT BELIEVING

You may wonder, "Why is there so much information on the Web? Who put it there?" Good questions! Every Web site tells a story. Some home pages are put up by people simply because they want to share everything they know about a certain subject with as many people as possible. Some Web pages are educational resources meant to serve the students at a particular school, and they just happen to be open to the public. Some others—well, okay, almost *all* of the others—are there because someone wants to make money from the information they have to offer. Don't let that put you off though. It shouldn't cost you anything to find an incredible amount of information for school online. Almost every web site is free, open, and available to everyone, although some pay for themselves by selling space on their home pages to advertisers—just like TV.

But be careful! Sometimes you get what you pay for. There are millions of home pages on the Web. For school and research purposes, 99 percent of them are practically useless. Any knucklehead can put up a Web page (and most of them do!) A lot of home pages are online versions of vanity license plates on cars. They do nothing more than shout "Look, Ma, I'm on the Web!" It's important to remember when looking for information online that just because it's on the Web doesn't make it true. People put up Web sites for all kinds of reasons. One of the skills necessary to be a supersearcher is figuring out how trustworthy is the information you've found. Does the person telling you something have a particular point of view that they're selling? Is there any reason you shouldn't trust their information? These are the kinds of questions reporters and researchers ask themselves all the time, especially if they're not familiar with the source of information. You should always try to make sure the information you find online is accurate and comes from a source you can trust!

SAFE AND SMART ON THE WEB

There's been lots of talk about "adult" content online. Understandably, this makes lots of parents and teachers nervous about letting kids roam around the Web by themselves. The reality is that hype about cyberporn and other X-rated or offensive content material gives a skewed picture of the amount of this kind of stuff out there. Still, it's important to take these concerns seriously, and there are steps that can be taken to insure the Web stays kid-friendly.

A number of schools are having students write up an "appropriate usage contract agreement" signed by kids and parents/guardians. This treats kids like grown-ups and asks them to guarantee on their honor that they will not visit sites intended for adults.

If that's not a strong enough solution, Web sites with adult content can be physically blocked by software packages that only allow access to a list of approved sites. There are a number of commercially available software packages that do this, including SurfWatch (SurfWatch Software), Cybersitter (Solid

Oak Software), Cyber Patrol and Net Blocker Plus (Microsystems Software), and Net Nanny (Net Nanny). If your parents think the Web is not where you belong, you might ask them if they're aware of these programs. Won't *they* be impressed?

REFERENCE HELP ON THE WEB

Once you're ready to surf the Web, and you've got the basics of navigation down, you'll find it's an unbelievable resource for school. Check out some of these cool sites for a quick sample of how fun and easy it is to find facts online.

KIDS WEB DIGITAL LIBRARY
(http://www.npac.syr.edu/textbook/kidsweb/)
The Kids Web Digital Library should be your first stop when digging for info on the Web. No matter what the subject—art, drama, literature, science, social studies, or just fun and games—the Digital Library organizes it all for you and points you in the right direction.

THE VIRTUAL REFERENCE DESK
(http://thorplus.lib.purdue.edu/reference/)
Purdue University put together this one-stop online reference resource with links to government Web sites, dictionaries, maps and travel information, science sites, news archives, and tons of other reference sources around the world.

BIOGRAPHICAL DICTIONARY
(http://www.tiac.net/users/parallax/)
If you're looking for quick facts about important men

and women in history, from ancient times to today, click here.

BARTLETT'S FAMILIAR QUOTATIONS
(http://www.columbia.edu/acis/bartleby/bartlett/)
Who said it? If you know a famous quote but don't know who said it, *Bartlett's* has the answer. Or if you're looking for the perfect quotation to put in your yearbook, consult the most comprehensive quote compendium on the Net. You can search by speaker, key word, or subject.

CIA WORLD FACT BOOK
(http://www.odci.gov/cia/publications/95fact/index.html)
You don't have to be a spy to use the *CIA World Fact Book.* It's one of the best, most comprehensive information resources on the Web. If you have a question about another country, you'll find the answer here—plus you'll find lots of great maps.

OTHER REFERENCE WORKS ON THE WEB

Acronym Dictionary
(gopher://info.mcc.ac.uk/77/miscellany/acronyms)

Online Dictionary of Computing
(http://wombat.doc.ic.ac.uk/)

Roget's Thesaurus
(gopher://odie.niaid.nih.gov:70/77/.thesaurus/index)

Strunk & White's Elements of Style
(http://www.cc.columbia.edu/acis/bartleby/strunk/)

Webster's Dictionary
(http://c.gp.cs.cmu.edu:5103/prog/webster)

MAKE YOUR OWN HOME PAGE ON THE WEB- - - - - - - - - - - - - - - - - -

Should you have your very own home page on the Web? A lot of people have put themselves in cyberspace, with home pages about, well, themselves! It's like publishing your very own magazine: You can design your home page to reflect your interests, hobbies, and artistic flair! If you're a horse fanatic, for example, you can devote your home page to facts you've learned about horses, stories about your riding adventures, and pictures of horses; you can also link out to other sites with information about horses. Your home page can be headquarters for a social cause you care about, such as homelessness, poverty, literacy. You can provide people with information—even rally support. Or you can build a home page for extra credit or for a school project. It's totally up to you!

To make a home page, you need a special account on the Web. In addition to access to the World Wide Web, you'll also need a special place reserved on your online service's system to keep your home page. Your parents should ask your online service if it offers server space for users' home pages (it's like renting space on the service's computers to house your home page). There may be an extra fee involved.

To make your own home page, you'll need to code the documents you want to put on your site using commands in hypertext markup language. Don't worry—you don't need to be a computer programmer to learn how to use HTML. You just need to know a few basic commands, or tags, which are actually pretty similar to the ones you use with your word processor to center, make bold, and indent text—only in HTML, words and pictures can hyperlink to whatever you like!

There are several good software programs that can take you through the tagging process step by step, or you can teach yourself how to tag and use your word processor to create HTML documents. Using special software can make the job easier and less time consuming, but, depending on the kind of online service you use, it can also be expensive. If you're a subscriber to America Online, you're in luck. They've just started to offer software called NaviPress that makes creating a home page as easy as pointing and clicking. If your computer is running Microsoft's Windows 95, you have a tool called Internet Assistant, which also makes creating HTML documents a breeze. Other services, however, may not provide you with home page–authoring software. That means you'll either have to teach yourself (with the help of a knowledgeable friend or family member and a good book) or buy special software yourself.

TIPS FOR MAKING YOUR HOME PAGE

If you're interested in learning more about building your own home page, you can get more information from your online service or at some of these Web sites.

A BEGINNER'S GUIDE TO HTML
(http://www.ncsa.uiuc.edu/General/Internet/WWW/HTMLPrimer.html)
This is a primer for producing documents in HTML, written by the folks who invented the language.

CASE WESTERN RESERVE UNIVERSITY'S
INTRODUCTION TO HTML
(http://www.cwru.edu/help/introHTML/toc.html)

This university in Ohio is world famous for its activity on the Internet and the Web, so they really know what they're talking about when it comes to HTML! They've complied this guide specifically for beginners.

THE HTML LEARNING CENTER
(http://wwwhome.elysian.net/~jglass/tutor/main.html)

Another good HTML tutorial, written by a plain old nice guy who wants to help beginners learn how to program in HTML. It's very easy to follow.

THE NEXT WAVE ON THE WEB

Things are moving quickly on the World Wide Web. While most of us are just discovering this amazing resource for the first time, software developers are already working overtime, trying to create the next big wave for cybersurfers.

Cable modem delivery. If you're used to AOL and commercial online services, you might find the Web annoyingly slow. That's because all its massive graphics and text, audio, and video files must be channeled through narrow phone lines. In the future (it's already happening in some test cities like Elmira, New York, and Akron, Ohio), you'll be able to get wired to the Net through cable television wires. Cable companies will simply split the cables, dedicating one to television and the other to computers. If you think of a phone line as a straw, a cable is like a firehose. It can deliver tons of data at lightning-fast speeds. This means you'll still be able to do all the things on the Web that you do now (deep database searches, chatting with pals, and more), but you'll also be able to see real-time animation and video and hear audio—you'll even be able to *see* your friends via real-time teleconferencing over the Internet.

Streaming sound and video. Now when you want to hear audio clips on the Net, you have to download a player first, then wait to download the sound file itself. In the next year, you'll be able to hear music, speeches—any kind of sound—on the fly (no more downloading) with streaming audio technology. It sends audio files in little packets of information— instead of in one superbig chunk—which are opened by a special application that sits in your computer, so the phone lines don't have to do all the work. For you, that means stereo sound on your computer! The same goes for video.

Java applets and apps. Java, a great program written by the folks at Sun Microsystems, is almost guaranteed to revolutionize the way people use the Net. It will help launch illustrated animations (imagine the Animaniacs playing pranks on your computer screen). It could also bring about a complete revolution in the computer industry by letting computer users treat the Internet as their hard drive—no more software compatibility problems.

3-D graphics. If you can't wait to enter virtual reality, VRML (virtual reality modeling language) is your ticket to ride! This programming language will put the "space" in cyberspace, rendering today's flat objects and landscapes in 3-D—you'll be able to fly-through online worlds, and create avatars that walk through "real" cities.

WANT TO KNOW MORE ABOUT THE WEB?

One of the best places to learn about the Web is on the Web itself. There are several terrific sites to help you learn your way around the Web and find cool, useful sites. Here's a few suggestions.

WORLD WIDE WEB WORKBOOK
(http://sln.fi.edu/primer/setup.html)
It's one thing to read about the Web and how it works. It's another to try it for yourself. If you're new to Web surfing, check out the World Wide Web Workbook from the Franklin Institute Science Museum. It's a series of Web pages that walks you step by step through how to use the Web—perfect for beginners!

NASA K–12
(http://quest.arc.nasa.gov/)
NASA has terrific resources for projects—especially if you want to study the Net itself!

LEARNING TOOL
(http://www.cs.uidaho.edu/~connie/
interests.html)
Connie Hatley is the senior secretary of the department of computer science at the University of Idaho. She has schools in mind with her Web site, The Web as a Learning Tool. Here you'll find links to educational sites of literature, art, music, science, history, and other subjects. There's even a section that will

point the way for you to design your own home page on the Web! Connie has reviewed many of the sites she points you toward, so she can save you from wasting a lot of time wandering around aimlessly. It's a neat, beginner-friendly site!

WEBWISE
(http://webwise.walcoff.com/)

"Just because it's on the Web," notes WebWise, "it doesn't necessarily mean it's good." This site, put up by the Washington, D.C., high-tech firm Walcoff & Associates, Inc., does a good job of pointing out what's worth seeing on the Web. Their library is especially useful for its list of links to online newspapers and magazines.

☛ **EXPERT TIP:** If you spend most of your time online on the Web, it might be a lot cheaper to switch from the commercial online services to a direct access Internet service such as AT&T WorldNet, where you pay a flat monthly fee of $19.95 instead of hourly connect charges. If you want the best of both, CompuServe's new WOW! service offers Web surfing and the comfortable surroundings of a kid-friendly commercial online service for the same price.

Subject by Subject

"I'm a freshman in high school. I use the online encyclopedia because it is so convenient and full of useful information. I have also e-mailed other teens for homework help and e-mailed them with my homework tips. Some of my classmates also have AOL so I e-mail them with homework information."

—MARCELLE YOUNG,
San Diego, CA

From astronomy to zoology, there's a corner of cyberspace devoted to your favorite school subject—and a place to find help with your toughest subject. "It is such a valuable resource for all of my classes," says Brandon Bruce, a senior at Cate School in Carpinteria, California, who was a delegate to the 1995 Global Information Infrastructure Junior Summit in Tokyo. "For economics I can get stock updates (quotes, graphs, predictions), for English I can learn about some of the classics like Shakespeare, for calculus I can research math history, for compsci I can investigate the newest computer languages like Java and VRML, for Spanish I can go to Web pages written in Spanish and get information on Spanish-speaking countries, and for multimedia graphics—well, you know how awesome the graphics on the Web are!"

With the help of hundreds of kids like Brandon and their teachers, we've compiled a list of dozens of classroom-tested Web sites and online areas that are terrific homework help resources! The subject-by-subject list in this chapter will help you find information on many different subjects quickly and easily.

Keep in mind, this list isn't meant to be complete or even comprehensive but to give you a taste of what's out there. There are thousands of Web sites on almost every imaginable topic, and listing them all would be a book by itself. A very *big* book. In fact, you could spend an awful lot of time cruising from site to site looking for help with a particular subject and getting very frustrated. This list will make your searches a little easier.

CYBERSPACE BY SUBJECT

AGRICULTURE
The World Wide Web Virtual Library: Agriculture (http://ipm_www.ncsu.edu/cernag/cern.html) serves up links to state and county departments of agriculture, safety information, institutes and colleges, farming weather, and many other links. Another terrific web resource is the **Plants Database Home Page** from the U.S. Department of Agriculture (http://plants.usda.gov/plants/). Fill out a form to find out more about a plant. It's useful if you want to know the scientific name of a plant, for example. You'll also

find information about rare, endangered, or threatened plants.

ANATOMY
One of the more bizarre and fascinating Internet stories is about convicted murderer and fitness freak Joseph Paul Jernigan. He was executed for his crime and donated his body to science. He was frozen solid and cut up with, well ... Lets just say he was cut into *very* thin slices. Jernigan is now known as Adam on the Internet. See **The Visible Human Project** (http://www.nlm.nih.gov/extramural_research.dir/ visible_human.html) to read all about it and see what you would look like if you fell into a giant deli slicer—1,800 times. Hey, science isn't always pretty, OK? The **Whole Brain Atlas** (http://count51.med. harvard.edu/AANLIB/home.html) features lots of pictures of different parts of the brain. **The Heart: A Virtual Exploration** (http://sln.fi.edu/biosci/biosci. html) takes you through the different areas of the heart and explains how it works.

ART
See Chapter Eight, "Museums and More in Cyberspace."

ASTRONOMY
America Online subscribers can learn about the basics of astronomy at the **Astronomy Club** (key word: Astronomy), hosted by the associate editor of *Sky and Telescope* magazine. **The National Space Society** (key word: Space), an educational nonprofit organization dedicated to the creation of a space-faring civilization, also maintains an area on AOL. CompuServe has a very active **Astronomy Forum** (GO ASTRO-

FORUM) devoted to skywatching as a profession and as a hobby. The forum is run by Dick DeLoach, who is a research scientist for NASA. You'll also find many professional astronomers and observatory and planetarium officials there.

The really deep resources for stargazers are on the Web, which has hundreds of sites devoted to astronomy. For basic information about the solar system, check out **The Nine Planets** (http://seds.lpl.arizona. edu/nineplanets/nineplanets/nineplanets.html), an award-winning Web site about our solar system. You'll find pictures from NASA spacecraft, sounds, and an occasional movie about each of the planets and major moons in our solar system. Unlike a lot of astronomy Web sites, which are intended for professional scientists, The Nine Planets was written with students in mind—there's even a helpful glossary of all technical and astronomical terms as well as links to more information elsewhere on the Web. Another great starting point is the **Astronomy Course for High School Students** (http://www.cnde. iastate.edu/staff/jtroeger/astronomy.html), which includes material on stargazing, observing the night sky, finding your way around the skies, the moon, sun, solar system, galaxies, quasars, cosmology, and more.

While you're lost in space, check our **Views of the Solar System** (http://bang.lanl.gov/solarsys/), an educational tour of the solar system, with over 200 pages of information and nearly 1,000 high-resolution images and animations, and over 840 megabytes of data. Travel through space simply by clicking on a desired planet. **View of the Moon** (http://saatel.shiny. it/users/lore/moon.html) shows the moon in its current phase and gives information about when the different phases of the moon occur. **Earth and Universe** (http://www.eia.brad.ac.uk/btl/) is also worth a visit. It's a comprehensive multimedia guide to the cosmos. The **Comet Observation Page** (http://encke. jpl.nasa.gov/) has information on visible comets and over 200 pictures of 26 different comets. The **Meteor Showers** home page (http://medicine.wustl.edu/ ~kronkg/meteor_shower.html) lists meteor showers by the month. **Meteoroids and Meteorites** (http:// bang.lanl.gov/solarsys/meteor.htm) is the place to view impact craters and images.

If virtual space travel doesn't do it for you, check our **Basics of Space Flight** (http://www.jpl.nasa. gov/basics/bsf2-2.htm#right). You'll find links to information needed for space flight—different parts of the solar system, the earth and its rotation and revolution, gravity, Newton's and Kepler's laws, interplanetary trajectories, planetary orbits, electromagnetic phenomena, experiments, spacecraft classification, telecommunications, onboard systems, science instruments, navigation, and lots more. Yes, it *is* rocket science. **Hubble Space Telescope Information Service** (http://www.stsci.edu/top.html) is the place to, well, find out more about the Hubble Space Telescope. Duh.

AVIATION

The WWW site **Flight** (http://smdg2.nmsi.ac.uk/ collexh/) features lots of information on early flight, including profiles of aviation pioneers and the earliest machines that flew. Don't miss **To Fly Is Everything** (http://hawaii.cogsci.uiuc.edu/invent/air planes.html), which covers the history of flight, including lots of photos. As you might guess, **Aviation Links** (http://www.cyberspace.com/mbrunk/

avlinks.html) offers plenty of links to online publications, aviation museums, airlines, airports, pictures, and more. Sooner or later, what goes up must come down. Visit **The Story of Gravity** (http://microgravity. msad.hq.nasa.gov/aIntro/gstory.html) and you'll be doubly impressed with what it takes to get airborne.

A good place to meet experts in flying is the **Aviation Forum** on AOL (key word: Aviation), which features information on everything from airshows to online conferences. **Flying** magazine also maintains a site on AOL (key word: Flying). One of the oldest virtual hangars online is CompuServe's Aviation Forum (GO AVSIG), where you'll find experts discussing every conceivable flight-related topic.

BIOLOGY

What's so cool about **The Interactive Frog Dissection** (http://curry.edschool.Virginia.EDU/~insttech/ frog)? Plenty. No scalpel, no formaldehyde, no more nervously peering out of the corner of your eye at your lab partner with the queasy stomach. This on-line tutorial walks you through all the good stuff— skin incisions, muscle incisions, and internal organs. Yum! You want more? Then you want the **Whole Frog Project** (http://george.lbl.gov/ITG.hm.pg. docs/Whole.Frog/Whole.Frog.html), featuring the skeleton, organs, and digestive and nervous systems of the frog. Pictures are labeled and can be enlarged for closer viewing. Don't miss the rotating frog movie. Wanna play virtual surgeon some more? It's the Cow's Eye Dissection (http://www.exploratorium. edu/learning_studio/cow_eye/), which features directions and photos for dissecting the eye of a cow.

Hey, you never know when you might need to know this stuff.

If you hope to get past tenth grade science, however, you'll definitely need to know the stuff covered in the hypertext book **Cell Biology** (http://esg-www. mit.edu:8001/esgbio/cb/cbdir.html), which covers cell basics, cell structure, and mitosis. Play mad scientist and learn about the rules of genetic inheritance in **The Virtual Fly Lab** (http://vflylab.calstatela. edu/edesktop/VirtApps/VflyLab/IntroVflyLab. html) by creating your own genetic cross between two fruit flies. Click on Designing a Cross and go to the genetics lab. Eeeaaaaggghh!!! It's alive!!

Biology is a topic in CompuServe's **Science/Math Education Forum** (GO SCIENCE). If you're an AOL subscriber, visit **Access Excellence** (key word: Excellence), which offers scientific information and classroom activities provided for and by high school biology teachers from around the country. On the Web, the **Access Excellence Resource Center** (http:// www. gene.com/ae/RC/) has an exhaustive collection of biology resources and hypertext links.

BOTANY

For our money, nothing says "cool science project" like flesh-eating plants. Leave the pea plants and genetic experiments to Gregor Mendel—he's, like, so one hundred years ago. Instead, get over to **The Carnivorous Plant FAQ** (http://astro.as.arizona.edu/ ~barry/cps/faq/faq.html) for answers to all kinds of questions about the Venus's-flytrap and other meat-eaters.

The **Fast Plants** Web site (http://fastplants.cals. wisc.edu) is great for students doing bio-lab projects using the "Fast Plants" system. Another good, basic resource is **The Complete Guide to Garden Stuff** from *Books That Work* (http://www.btw.com/garden_archive/toc.html), which has detailed information on soils, mulch and grass, fertilizers, pest control, gardening tools, and seed starting and growing. Don't want to get your hands dirty? Then surf over to **The Tele-Gardener** (http://www.usc.edu/dept/garden/) and have a robot plant a seed in the garden for you. Don't forget to tell it to water.

CHEMISTRY
Chemistry Index (http://www.chem.vt.edu/sci-index.html) is a terrific site! It features an alphabetical listing of all sorts of chemical terms, laws, and applications. "It is like having a chemistry encyclopedia on your desk," raves one teacher. Wait a minute. Wouldn't that take up less space than a computer? Anyway, it also has hypertext links to areas where chemistry terms are explained with plenty of diagrams.

Looking for an online periodic table for chemistry class? There are several cool interactive tables on the Web. **Periodic Table** (http://www.cs.ubc.ca/elements/periodic-table) is simple to use, with the elements listed by symbol and atomic number. Click on the symbol and it leads to a list of several pieces of information on each element. The **Los Alamos National Lab** (http://www-c8.lanl.gov/infosys/html/periodic/periodic.html) has a terrific full-color periodic table. Click on the symbol found on the picture of the periodic table, and it will lead to more information about that element. **Elementistory** (http://www.dmu.ac.uk/~sfairall/periodic/elementi.html) gives the history behind all the elements, while **Web-Elements** (http://www.shef.ac.uk/~chem/

web-elements/genr-nt/periodic-table.html), another good Web resource, also offers information on each element and a periodic table.

EARTH SCIENCE

Earth Science Resources on the Internet (http://www. geosci.unc.edu/web/ESresources/ES12795.html) was set up for students at the University of North Carolina, Chapel Hill. It features simple instructions on how to find earth science–related info on the Internet. It also features a short list of hypertext links to other resources and organizations, including NASA's **Mission to Planet Earth** (http://spso.gsfc.nasa.gov/eos _edu.pack/toc.html), which is a global observation system examining the changes in the atmosphere, land, and oceans as a result of human activities.

ENERGY AND ELECTRICITY

You'll find lots of great science project and research ideas in **Geothermal Energy** (http://solstice.crest. org/renewables/re-kiosk/geothermal/index.shtml), which discusses how energy is generated by the earth. A connected Web site on **Hydro Energy** (http:// solstice.crest.org/renewables/re-kiosk/hydro/ index.shtml) teaches about getting energy from moving water, while **Solar Energy** (http://solstice.crest. org/renewables/re-kiosk/solar/index.shtml) is all about getting power from the sun. The **Mr. Solar Home Page** (http://www.netins.net/showcase/solar catalog/) has lots of information, with one hundred articles on all kinds of alternative energy, while **The Solar Cooking Archieve** (http://www.accessone. com/~sbcn/index.htm) gives directions for making your own solar cooker.

That covers water, sun, and underground energy

sources. Still not satisfied? Check out **Wind Power** (http://solstice.crest.org/renewables/re-kiosk/ wind/index.shtml). Want to build a small electric motor? Learn how at **Beakman's Electric Motor** (http://fly.hiwaay.net:80/~palmer/motor.html), which offers instructions. Once you build it, if you want an explanation on how it works, point your browser at **Electricity and Ben Franklin** (http://web 66.coled.umn.edu/hillside/franklin/jummy/ Project.html), which discusses the life of Ben Franklin and how he worked with electricity. Another good basic source of information is **Electricity** (http://ericir. syr.edu/Newton/Lessons/electric.html), which has lots of experiments you can get all charged up about.

ENGINEERING
"London Bridge is falling down, falling down, falling down." You probably sang that nursery rhyme when you were little. But do you remember the second verse? "Set a man to watch all night, watch all night, watch all night"? According to **Bridge Engineering** by Newton's Apple (http://ericir.syr.edu/Newton/ Lessons/bridges.html), "people once felt that a bridge required a human spirit. They sometimes buried a human sacrifice in the bridge's foundation, so that the spirit could 'watch all night.' " And to think that all this time I thought the bad smell at the foot of the Brooklyn Bridge was the Fulton Fish Market. But I digress. It's a great Web site at which to learn how engineers build bridges. If you want to know *why* engineers build bridges (to get to the other side?) ask one at the **Bridge Engineering Home Page** (http:// www.best.com/~solvers/bridge.html).

ENGLISH

Do visions of Pulitzer Prizes dance in your head? OK, maybe you just want to pass English composition. No matter what your literary ambitions, a visit to the **Trinity College Writing Center** (http://www.trincoll.edu/writcent/aksmith.html) can help sharpen your style. This Web resource keeps such desk reference classics as *Webster's Dictionary*, *Roget's Thesaurus*, and *Bartlett's Familiar Quotations* just a mouse click away. And for those occasional grammatical lapses, *Elements of Style* is indispensable. You also can read tips on revising and editing, learn how to cite electronic sources for articles or research papers, and skim "a zillion handouts" from Purdue University that range from exercises for eliminating wordiness (like the bridge story above) to a primer on nonsexist language. You' ll also find links to other online writing centers and student publications, and more. Trinity students can look forward to online tutoring here, but the rest of us have to go back to memorizing "*i* before *e* except after . . ."

Another cool composition helper is **Writing Tips, Guides, and Advice** (http://www.missouri.edu/~wleric/writehelp.html), which has lots of hints, suggestions, and links sure to beat the worst case of writer's block. English is a favorite topic in CompuServe's **Education Forum** (GO EDFORUM) as well.

ENTOMOLOGY

A fancy word for a cool subject: bugs. The tour begins at **B-Eye: The World Through the Eyes of a Bee** (http://cvs.anu.edu.au/andy/beye/beyehome.html), which will make you wonder why bees don't fly into things more often. **Arachnology** (http://dns.ufsia.

ac.be/Arachnology/Arachnology.html) links to a variety of information on spiders, while the **Entomology Home Page** (gopher://bluehen.ags.udel.edu:71/hh/.insects/.descriptions/entohome.html) is an insect database with information on seventeen different orders of insects.

Attention, gross-out fans: How can you resist **Cockroach World: The Yuckiest Site on the Internet** (http://www.nj.com/yucky/roaches/index.html), which has lots of cool pictures, "A Day in the Life of a Cockroach," how to catch and keep cockroaches (er, no thanks), and everything you could want to know about our friend the cockroach. OK, maybe more than you want to know. More bugs? Check out the **University of Florida** *Book of Insect Records* (http://gnv.ifas.ufl.edu/~tjw/recbk.htm) for sixteen bug records: fastest flier, most tolerant of cold, smallest eggs, fastest wing beat, and most spectacular mating. Spice up that report with downloaded pictures of beetles, lice, mosquitoes, and ticks from the **Entomology Image Gallery** (http://www.public.iastate.edu/~entomology/ImageGallery.html).

Bet you think we're making this one up: **Insect Recipes** from Kentucky University (http://www.uky.edu/Agriculture/Entomology/ythfacts/entyouth.html) is Scott O'Grady's favorite home page. Lots of tasty information including: bugfood I and II, bug olympics, butterflies, camouflage, classroom mascots, collecting insects, making your own compound eye, bug jokes, bug riddles, and how insects eat. Bon appètit!

ENVIRONMENT
AOL members can start their search for info on the environment at the **Environmental Club** (key word: Earth), which features lots of up-to-date news, active

message boards, and links to Web sites. Environmental issues are also the main subject of CompuServe's **Earth Forum** (GO EARTH), which is run by an editor at *Field & Stream* magazine. You'll also meet environmental scientists and professionals, media people, and experts from a number of environmental organizations.

Global Warming (http://www.ncdc.noaa.gov/gblwrmupd/global.html) has the latest information on global warming and terrific graphs showing trends in different areas. **Science and the Environment** (http://www.voyagepub.com/publish/chapters.htm) offers a big selection of news stories about different environmental issues from a variety of newspapers and magazines. The **Endangered Species Home Page** (http://nceet.snre.umich.edu/EndSpp/Endangered.html) tells all about endangered or extinct animals, with fact sheets, pictures, maps, and copies of laws that affect endangered animals. **The Internet Environmental Library** (http://envirolink.org/envirowebs.html) has links to environmental sites with information on how people can affect the environment. **Forty Tips to Go Green** (http://www.ncb.gov.sg/jkj/env/greentips.html) has lots of conservation advice.

GEOGRAPHY

A fun site on the Web is called **How Far Is It?** (http://www.indo.com/distance/). It tells you the precise distance between any two places in the United States. Say you're in Tulsa and your key pal is in Tuscaloosa. Enter in the two cities and you'll find out that you're exactly 521 miles apart. It can also tell you the longitude and latitude of each city. Click on a map and see where those two cities are located. Click again and zoom in for a closer look. **Map Maker** (http://loki.ur.utk.edu/ut2Kids/maps/map.html) is cartography made easy—lots of info on how maps are made. The **Earth Viewer** (http://www.fourmilabl.ch/earthview/vplanet.html) lets you look at the earth from many different views. Let there be light! With a mouse click, you can make it day or night, check out the earth from the sun, the moon, or any spot above the earth determined by longitude and latitude.

The commercial online services offer several good geography resources, too. **National Geographic Online** on AOL (key words: NGS, Geographic) is a rich resource, featuring *National Geographic* articles, a Kids Network area with a message board and conference hall for members to communicate, and libraries for projects and lesson plans. The **Student Forum** on CompuServe (GO STUDENTS) also has an active geography area.

GEOLOGY

The **U.S. Geological Survey** Web site (http://info.er.usgs.gov/) offers access to the government's many geology, maps, and water resources. There's a whole lotta shakin' going on at **Earthquake Statistics** (http://info.er.usgs.gov/data/geologic/neic/lists/index.html), where you'll find information on past earthquakes, significant U.S. quakes, the most destructive earthquakes, facts and statistics, and the number of earthquakes per year with a magnitude of seven or more on the Richter scale. The **Earthquake Fact Sheet** (http://www.fema.gov/fema/quakef.html) gives information on what to do before, during, and after an earthquake. If you want to shake *and* bake, pay a visit or **Volcano World** (http://volcano.

und.nodak.edu/), which is a great starting point for volcanology: volcanoes of the world, volcanic parks and monuments, learning about volcanoes, and "ask a volcanologist." **The Electronic Volcano** (http://www.dartmouth.edu/pages/rox/volcanoes/elecvolc.html) is another place for information on active volcanoes, including pictures, maps, and volcanic observatories.

Step back in time—way back—in the **Geological Time Machine** (http://ucmp1.berkeley.edu/time form.html) and visit twenty-six different time periods, from the Precambrian to the Quaternary. **Evolution Entrance** (http://ucmp1.berkeley.edu/exhibittext/evolution.html) looks at the history of evolution, including Charles Darwin and some of the early scientists involved in evolution. **The Fossil Company Picture Gallery** (http://www.gold.net/users/dt89/gallery.html) is loaded with pictures of a wide variety of fossils and features a terrific collection of links to Internet sites about fossils. Lastly, check out the **Rockhounds Information Page** (http://www.rahul.net/infodyn/rockhounds/rockhounds.html) for links to a variety of related sites. It rocks.

GEOMETRY

Whether you love geometry or hate it, **The Geometry Forum** (http://forum.swarthmore.edu) is for you. This site features a student center with a geometry problem of the week, cool ideas for projects, and Ask Dr. Math, which lets you get help with geometry and other math problems via e-mail. You can take advantage of this feature even if you don't have Web access. Just e-mail your question to dr.math@forum.swarthmore.edu.

GOVERNMENT AND POLITICS

Take a virtual tour of the White House, learn about the executive branch of the government, and meet the first family at the **Welcome to the White House** home page (http://www.whitehouse.gov). You can even hear a sound file of Socks, the first cat, meowing. Learn everything you could want to know about Congress at **Thomas** (http://thomas.loc.gov), a service of the Library of Congress. You can look up a summary and the status of every piece of legislation before the House and Senate, lists of hot bills before Congress, and the full text of the *Congressional Record.* You'll also find a copy of the Constitution and information on how laws are made. It's called Thomas after Thomas Jefferson. Congress apparently thought that sounded more dignified than NewtNet. You can follow campaign '96 up close on **AllPolitics** (http://allpolitics.com) from *Time* magazine and CNN.

You can always find an argument—er, discussion—about politics on the commercial online services. On AOL, visit **The Capital Connection** (key words: Capital, Politics, Government, Debate, Issues), which unites all of America Online's political and government forums, including **Washington Agenda, Washington Week in Review,** and **C-SPAN.** In addition, Capital Connection features e-mail addresses of politicians, the latest information from state and local candidates, and a guide to politics on the Internet. On CompuServe, check out the **Political Debate Forum** (GO POLITICS). If you like to look at things from the right or the left, go to the **Republican Forum** (GO REPUBLICAN) or **Democratic Party Forum** (GO DEMOCRATS). Party on!

HEALTH

AOL's **Better Health and Medical Forum** (key words: Health, Medicine) is for both consumers and health professionals. You can use the message boards to contact health and medical experts and find everything you need to know about most major illnesses. CompuServe has enormous health resources including the **Health Database Plus** (GO HLTDB), a premium service that charges extra for articles you download from tons of different health-related publications. They also offer the **Health and Fitness Forum** (GO GOODHEALTH); **HealthNet** (GO HNT); and **MedSig** (GO MEDSIG), a forum for health professionals—a good place to look for expert help.

Kevin's Food Guide Pyramid Page (http://www. ksu.edu/~kknight/nutrition.html) explains the food pyramid and how many servings are needed of each food group. **A Comprehensive Guide to First Aid** from the British Red Cross (http://pharmweb1.man. ac.uk/redcross/firstaid.html) offers basic steps for first aid in common situations. The **Centers for Disease Control** (http://www.cdc.gov) has information on diseases, health risks, scientific data, and health statistics. The **Wellness** (http://www.hsc.ufl.edu/hs/ wellness.htm) site is a collection of answers to health questions by Dr. Patrick J. Bird, dean of the College of Health and Human Performance at the University of Florida. Wanna play doctor? At **The Interactive Patient** (http://medicus.marshall.edu/medicus.htm) you are given the case history of a patient. You can do a physical exam, get lab and X-ray results, and then make a diagnosis. Best of all, you can't be sued for malpractice.

HISTORY

One of the things online services and the Internet do best is store electronic documents. So some of the richest treasure troves online are about history. On America Online, **The Atlantic Monthly** (key word: Atlantic) has a unique feature called Flashbacks and Follow-ups. *The Atlantic* has been publishing for nearly 150 years. They regularly go through their archives and post long-forgotten articles that shed light on what's going on today. You think the O. J. Simpson trial was " the trial of the century?" Go back and read all about the 1927 trial of Sacco and Vanzetti in Boston. Doing a report on the effects of smoking? Perhaps you'd be interested in an article from 1860 that shows the debate was just as strong more than 135 years ago. Elsewhere on AOL, the **History** message board (key word: History) is a great place to leave research questions.

On Prodigy, check out *America Heritage* **Online** (jump: *American Heritage*), which has a historic photos library. On CompuServe, military history is the subject in **The Military Forum** (GO MILITARY). The **Living History Forum** (GO LIVING) is a place to learn about reenactment and Renaissance fairs.

One of the most popular American history Web sites is **From Revolution to Reconstruction** (http://grid.let.rug.nl/~welling/usa/revolution.html). Despite the name, it's now been updated well into the twentieth century. **The Civil War Homepage** (http://cobweb.utcc.utk.edu/~hoemann/warweb.html) is one of the best history resources we've come across online. It features a time line of the Civil War, links to thousands of pictures, information about specific battles, diaries and letters from soldiers, and much more. **Historic Documents** (http://www.ukans.edu/carrie/docs/docs_us.html) features the complete text of many important documents in U.S. history, like the Iroquois constitution, the Declaration of Independence, the Proclamation of First Thanksgiving, and many others. The **Gateway to World History** (http://neal.ctstateu.edu/history/world_history/index.html) is a super site with *tons* of links to other history sites!

LANGUAGE

Jacques Léon of Montreal, Canada, is not a teacher, but he has posted the **French Lesson Home Page** (http://teleglobe.ca/~leo/french.html) because, "I know my own language well enough to be able to teach it." Don't you love the French? For French addicts, a **French Page** (http://www.acs.appstate.edu/~griffinw/website/french.html) maintained by Appalachian State University provides valuable information on French Web resources around the world. Spanish students can point their browsers at **Web Spanish Lessons** (http://www.willamette.edu/~tjones/Spanish/Spanish-main.html).

German students can find a handy, searchable **German-English Dictionary** at (http://www.tu-chemnitz.de/~fri/forms/dict.html). If you're taking Japanese, check out **Japanese Language Learning Cyber-Tutorials** (http://www.twics.com/~kenbutler/learning.html). If it's help with Russian you want, then head for the Web's **Russian Language Course** (http://solar.rtd.utk.edu/oldfriends/language/course/school.html). **The Virtual Library: Languages** (http://www.willamette.edu/~tjones/languages/WWW_Virtual_Library_Language.html) has pointers to Web sites on *every* other language you can imagine.

Lots of colleges have an off-campus international house, where students of many nationalities live together, celebrate one another's holidays and cuisines, and study one another's native tongues. AOL has adopted this concept for it's own **International House** (key words: Classes; ies), devoted to second languages and knowledge of other cultures. A different language is spoken every night, offering a fun opportunity to practice without having to search for partners or feel self-conscious. CompuServe's **Foreign Language Forum** (GO FLEFO) is for teachers and students of all languages. Question: If CompuServe is available all over the world, which languages are foreign to it?

LITERATURE

Barrons' Booknotes on America Online (key word: Booknotes) offers more than one hundred guides to great works of literature, from *The Aeneid* to *Wuthering Heights*. Each edition has biographies of the author; plot summaries; descriptions and analyses of characters, themes, settings, and literary devices; and more. A major butt saver.

If you think the play's the thing, then you will love **The Complete Works of William Shakespeare** (http://the-tech.mit.edu/Shakespeare/works.html). The full text of each of Shakespeare's histories, comedies, and tragedies is here in a fully searchable digital form. Who said, "To be or not to be?" You can look it up in seconds. You can also join a discussion of the Bard's works, search for familiar quotations from his plays, and link to other Shakespeare resources on the Internet. **The English Server** (http://english-www.hss.cmu.edu/) at Carnegie-Mellon University is a terrific resource for students of all forms of literature, especially the **Drama Server,** which contains a number of plays, screenplays, and discussions of drama and dramatic productions.

Another terrific Web site for information about literature is **The On-line Books Page** (http://www.cs.cmu.edu/Web/books.html). It features an index of over a thousand online books and exhaustive lists of links to other places to find books online. It also helps you find book publishers and retailers, online reference works, and electronic libraries. This is one page you'll definitely want to bookmark.

MATH

Do you think that math is mostly about numbers? Think you're no good at math? Think again. Visit **MegaMath** (http://www.c3.lanl.gov/mega-math), and you'll quickly see there are so many different topics in mathematics that everyone can find something that they like *and* that they're good at. The topics in MegaMath run from graphs and games to coloring. Bet you never thought of a box of Crayolas as a math problem, did you? Did you know it took mathematicians until 1976 to scientifically prove that you need just four different colors to draw a map of the world so that no two countries sharing a boundary will have the same color? MegaMath is full of the newest discoveries and hottest topics in mathematics, and you will see that these are easy to understand and fun to play around with.

You can get to lots of other math sites by pointing your browser at the **KidsWeb Math Page** (http://www.npac.syr.edu/textbook/kidsweb/math.html). And if you are a confirmed math lover, you can get on a mailing list that will send you a new math trick every week. Just send your request to BEATCALC @aol.com. **Internet Center for Mathematics Prob-**

lems (http://www.mathpro.com/math/mathCenter. html) is a listing of links to mathematics problem-solving areas of the Net, including the **Algebra Problem of the Week** (http://sasd.K12.pa.US/homepages/ AlgebraPOW) and the **On-line Mathematics Dictionary** (http://www.mathpro.com/math/glossary/ glossary.html), a large dictionary on math terms.

METEOROLOGY

Learn all about hurricanes and download satellite pictures, maps, and more at the National Hurricane Center's **Tropical Prediction Center** (http:// www.nhc.noaa.gov/index.html). The NHC keeps a weather eye out for tropical cyclones over the Atlantic, Caribbean, Gulf of Mexico, and the eastern Pacific, and distributes hurricane watches and warnings to the general public. **WebWeather** (http:// www.princeton.edu/Webweather/ww.html) lets you find the weather forecast for any city or state quickly and easily, while **INTELLiCast: USA Weather** (http://www.intellicast.com/weather/usa/) has a wide range of colorful maps, including radar, precipitation, and satellite maps. There are forecast maps for twenty-fours hours, forty-eight hours, and seventy-two hours, and weather information for major cities. The University of Illinois's **Weather World** (http://www.atmos.uiuc.edu/wxworld/html/ general.html) shows you infrared satellite images, visible satellite images, surface weather maps, and other cool stuff. Doing a report on tornadoes? Get to **Tornadoes** (http://cc.usu.edu/~kforsyth/Tornado. html) for information on how they're formed and rated.

OCEANOGRAPHY

Ocean Planet Home Page (http://seawifs.gsfc.nasa. gov/ocean_planet.html) is a Smithsonian Institution site that explains the ocean. **The Jason Project** (http://seawifs.gsfc.nasa.gov/JASON/HTML/MISSION_home.html) is an annual ocean expedition you can follow on your computer. **AquaNet** (http://www.aquanet.com/aquanet/) features a wide variety of oceanography material, including aquaculture, conservation, fisheries, maritime heritage, marine science, ocean engineering and technology, seafood, and related publications. (Isn't Aqua Net the name of a hair spray?) The **Underwater World Home Page** (http://pathfinder.com/@@j@l6TVHPogAAQK15/pathfinder/kidstuff/underwater/index.html) has lots of information for kids on what goes on beneath the waves. The **World Wide Web Virtual Fish Library** (http://www.actwin.com/WWWVL-Fish.html) is a huge listing of links to many fish sites, including aquariums, ichthyology, aquatic environmentalism, fishing as a sport, and more. The **Fish Information Service (FINS) Index** (http://www.actwin.com/fish) has complete information on freshwater and marine fish for the aquarium, plans for aquariums, aquarium plants, and diseases found in aquariums. Thar' she blows! **Whales on the Net** (http://whales.magna.com.au/home.html) has information on a variety of whales, whaling history, whales in the news, and whale watching. And just when you thought it was safe to go back on the Web, **The Great White Shark** (http://www.netzone.com/~drewgrgich/shark.html) features information on the sea's deadliest predator.

PALEONTOLOGY

The World Wide Web is dino heaven. **Funky Dinosaur Land** (http://www.comet.net/dinosaur/) has lots of articles on dinosaurs and dozens of links to dino info on the Web. You can tour **Dinosaur Hall** (http://ucmp1.berkeley.edu/exhibittext/dinosaur. html) at the University of California at Berkeley, or prowl through the **Dinosaurs in Hawaii Exhibition** (http://www.hcc.hawaii.edu/dinos/dinos. 1.html), which features pictures of bones from several dinosaurs. Some of the best dino pictures in cyberspace are at **The Dinosaur World Tour** (http://www. fleethouse.com/dinosaur/dino-vir.htm).

See Chapter Eight, "Museums and More in Cyberspace" for addresses of natural history museums and other Web sites with dinosaur exhibits.

PHYSICS

If you don't think physics can be fun, check out **The Particle Adventure—"An Interactive Tour of the Inner Workings of the Atom and the Tools for Discovery"** (http://www-pdg.lbl.gov/cpep/adventure. html)—a fun site all about the history of the atom, including current atomic theories. **About Temperature** (http://unidata.ucar.edu/staff/blynds/tmp. html) has information on the development of thermometers and temperature scales, heat and thermodynamics, kinetic theory, thermal radiation, and the temperature of the universe. If that shed more heat than light, go to **Optics for Kids** (http://www. opticalres.com/kidoptx.html), which has lots of information on light, lenses, and lasers, with plenty of great diagrams. **How Light Works** (http://curry. edschool.Virginia.edu/murray/Light/How_Light_ Works.html) explains all about white light, the spectrum, rainbows, refraction—it even tells you why roses are red. If you still can't see straight, check out the **Kaleidoscope Resource** (http://www.eiu. edu/ac/busi/lum/kr.html) for information on making kaleidoscopes and where to get the supplies. **The Science of Magnets** (http://buerkle.arc.leon.k12.fl.us/MAG/magtext.pg14.html) tells all about the forces involved in magnets and how they're used in science. And when all else fails, you can **Ask Dr. Neutrino** (http://nike.phy.bris.ac.uk/dr/ask.html) or check out the answers to past physics questions.

RELIGION

On AOL, visit the **Ethics & Religion Club** (key word: Religion), where members discuss religious and ethical issues that face today's society. CompuServe also has a very active **Religion Forum** (GO RELIGION), covering every active faith. On the Web, the most comprehensive resource is **Facets of Religion** (http://marvin.biologie.uni-freiburg.de/~amueller/religion/), part of the WWW Virtual Library. It's an extremely thorough and well-maintained list of online resources for all the world's major religions—and many smaller ones.

SCIENCE

On AOL, stop by the National Academy of Sciences' **NAS Online** (key word: NAS), featuring a database of articles on a wide variety of topics, including space, agriculture, technology, earth sciences, engineering. medicine, biology, chemistry, math, and information on public policy. There's also a conference area and text and graphics files for downloading. The magazine *Scientific American* (key word: Science) also maintains an area on AOL with current articles, recent back issues, and much more. Another good general interest area is **The Discovery Channel** and **The Learning Channel Online** (key words: Discovery, TLC). Science and technology are also the topics of discussion in CompuServe's **Mensa Forum** (GO MENSA) and **Students' Forum** (GO STUFO).

You Can with Beakman and Jax (http://www.nbn. com:80/youcan/index.html) offers answers to a whole range of weird science questions like "Is it true that Jell-O is made out of cow hooves?" The commonsense answer is: "Yes, we do get gelatin from dead animal skins and bones. But hamburgers come from dead animals, too." Hmm. I never thought of it that way. You even find serious, easy-to-understand scientific answers to gross-out questions like "Why do feet smell?" and "Where do farts come from?" (I can hear it now: But, Mom, it's my *science* project!) Go to **World Wide Web Links and Pointers** (http://www.aip.org/aip/wwwinfo.html) for links to a number of different sites on the physical sciences.

SOCIAL STUDIES

A terrific web resource is **B.E.S.S.T.** (http://www. halcyon.com/garycres/sshp/startup.html), which stands for Building Excellence in Social Studies through Technology. The page has been designed to help teachers and students explore the Net. There's an emphasis on the state of Washington here, but you'll find it useful no matter where you're from. It's updated weekly with new URLs, news, and events pertaining to social studies. (Also see "History," page 97).

ZOOLOGY

There are plenty of pictures and lots of interesting, fun facts about many major species of animals in the **Animal Information Database** (hhtp://www.bev.

net/education/SeaWorld/infobook.html) run by Sea
World. If you're seriously into animals, one of the
biggest resources on the Net is **The Electronic Zoo**
(http://netvet.wustl.edu/e-zoo.htm). It's the work of
"Net vet" Ken Boschart at Washington University in
St. Louis. Click on the animal icon for a huge set of
links to lots of different animals. Also worth a visit is
Kingdom Animalia (http://www.oit.itd.umich.edu/
bio108/Animalia.html), which starts out with the animal kingdom and breaks it down into ever smaller
groups. Gross out your sister with **Snakes of North
America** (http://www-personal.umich.edu/
~grussell/Project/snakes.html). If you take your reptiles (herpetology) seriously, then Australia's **AERG
Herp Page** (http://lake.canberra.edu.au/pub/aerg/
herps/hphome.htm) is for you. And don't miss **Bat
Conservation International** (http://www.batcon.
org/) for answers about bat houses, bat facts, bat
trivia, and secrets of photographing bats. You'll go
bat guano.

MORE WEB RESOURCES

Can't find what you're looking for in the list in this
chapter? Check out some of the following Web pages
that contain links to lots more sites!

JENNA BURRELL'S COOL AND USEFUL STUDENT RESOURCES
(http://www.teleport.com/~burrell/)
Jenna is a seventeen-year-old who has put together
a collection of interesting, understandable, and informative resource pages throughout the World Wide
Web. She's provided links to many of the sites mentioned in this chapter, and to dozens more on fine

arts and art history, literature, writing, foreign languages, science, mathematics, history and social studies, geography, government, and economics for high school students who want to use the Web to do research for school projects. "Most of the links that are listed lead to an actual source of information rather than just another directory," says Jenna. Bookmark this one!

INTERNET RESOURCES FOR THE K–12 CLASSROOM
(http://www.ncsa.uiuc.edu/Edu/Classroom/k12/)
A great toolbox from the National Center for Supercomputing Applications (NCSA), located at the University of Illinois at Urbana Champaign, has lots of links to Web sites on physical sciences (astronomy, physics, chemistry), social sciences (history, economics, government), and much more!

THE VOSE SCHOOL EDUCATIONAL RESOURCES
(http://www.teleport.com/~vincer/starter.html)
A great Web starting point, the Vose School site guides you to every school resource you could want, all organized by subject (humanities, science, etc.). This page was created by a teacher in Beaverton, Oregon, to introduce students and teachers to the Internet, so it's really easy to understand and use!

TAENA'S HOMEWORK HELPER
(http://www.norwest.com)
This is a commercial Web site, set up by Norwest Financial Services. What banking has to do with homework help beats me, but someone there has done a terrific job of setting up this Web resource for kids. They've surfed around and found lots of terrific

and useful Web sites—including many that don't show up on lots of similar lists. Best of all, they give capsule reviews of all the educational sites they point you to, so you can go right to the most useful sites. But here's one question they don't answer: Who—or *what*—is Taena?

SURF ON!

Keep in mind, the Web is growing every day. Web sites and home pages come and go all the time. They shut down or change addresses with little or no warning. That means any list of Web sites, including this one, can get outdated. If the URL you have for a specific site doesn't work, try entering the name of the Web site in Yahoo or Lycos—the site may have just moved. And try searching for sites not listed in this chapter. Cool new sites are coming online everyday!

Extra Help Online

"When I applied to colleges last year, I told them in my essays that working in telecommunications was the single most educational experience of my high school years. Though this may not have pleased my calculus teacher who never could get me to find the integral of x^2 properly, it's true. I don't know how I would view the world right now if I hadn't had daily contact with my friends around the globe."

—CELESTE PERRI,
Cold Spring Harbor High School

Maybe you've heard your grandparents whine about how they had to walk seven miles through the snow to get to school? Years from now the grandkids of AOL subscriber Joellen Schneider, a senior at Queen of Peace High School in Chicago, will probably roll their eyes and look bored when she describes for the umpteenth time how she used to boot up her computer to trudge through cyberspace to go to the on-line library. "It's the middle of February. There is a blizzard outside your window," she recalled. "You have to get information on the circulatory system. Do you risk your life and try to go the library? No way. You just sign on and use the online encyclopedia and browse through magazines.

"Imagine that it is nine o'clock on the night before your pre-calc homework is due and you have no clue how to do it," said Joellen. "That happened to me, but I just went to the homework help room and one of the teachers there helped me with the problems I didn't understand and taught me how to do them. It was great!"

AMERICA ONLINE'S ACADEMIC ASSISTANCE CENTER

"You are wonderful! You saved my life!" gushed a grateful student. "I guess I wasn't looking in the right places for my information. You really know your stuff!" Another satisfied customer of America Online's Academic Assistance Center (AAC).

Not too long ago, back in the days when the web was where you'd go to find spiders, you were lucky if your online service offered a searchable encyclopedia. Today, the commercial online services are duking it out to provide the best tools for online learning. One of the coolest—and busiest—online homework help services is offered by America Online. The Academic Assistance Center (key word: AAC) is staffed by over nine hundred online teachers who are always ready to lend a helping hand. There are even teacher pagers that put you in touch with real classroom teachers who man the computer keyboard around the clock to help you with brain-busting homework problems.

There are many ways to take advantage of AAC's

homework help. The best way to start is by clicking on Knowledge Database. This is a fully searchable collection of the hundreds of answers the Academic Assistance Center has given out in the last few years. You'd be surprised how often your exact question has already been asked and answered. Type in the topic you want to know more about—say, pollution—and the subject area (in this case, science) and click on Search the Database.

Another way to look for help is by posting your question in the Academic message boards. Teachers cruise these message boards dozens of times a day, offering helpful advice on where to turn for answers to homework questions, suggesting helpful resources online and off for research projects. Here's how it works.

This message was posted in AAC's History folder.

Subj: Nathan Bedford Forrest
Date: 96-01-06 14:16:03 EST
From: Sammy3631
Posted on: America Online

I need some help with a term paper on Nathan Bedford Forrest. Any help would be appreciated!

A short time later, an AAC teacher came to Sammy's rescue!

Subj: Re:Nathan Bedford Forrest
Date: 96-01-08 02:35:09 EST
From: MsPolish
Posted on: America Online

Nathan Bedford Forrest, 1821–1877, was one of the military geniuses of American history. He was the greatest cavalry leader in American history and the only officer on either side of the

Civil War to rise to a high rank without formal education. He raised and equipped cavalry at his own expense. Some of his command were involved in the Fort Pillow massacre. Forrest was accused of being personally responsible, but this later proved to be untrue. He died at Memphis, Tennessee, on October 29, 1877.

For more information please use key word WEB and check the following addresses:
http://www.aidt.edu/MontCtr/StJames/nbf.html
http://jackson.freenet.org/jfn/exchange/shiloh.html

Is that cool or what?

You'll notice it took more than twenty-four hours for Sammy to get his question about Nathan Bedford Forrest answered. That's fine if you're doing a research paper and have a few weeks. But if you're absolutely, positively stumped and you need help *right now*, go to one of the Academic Assistance classrooms. "When you get there, there are categories for you to pick from," says Joellen Schneider. "For example, math, science, or English. You click on the subject you need help in and *WHAM!* you're in a room with teachers who can help you. It takes about ten seconds to get a teacher to help you." Joellen is exaggerating a bit. It takes a *little* more than ten seconds. Each of these live chat classrooms is staffed every day between 4:00 P.M. and 2:00 A.M. Eastern time. They can get busy, but if you wait your turn, you will get help.

TEACHER PAGER

Another way to get homework help on AOL is through the teacher pager, which automatically sends e-mail to an online teacher who will help you with your question. AAC promises an answer within forty-eight hours, but it usually takes a lot less time than that.

Simply click your mouse on Teacher Pager on your screen. That will take you to separate pagers for math, science, English and languages, and history questions. Click on the subject you want, type your question, fill in your grade level, then hit Send. That's it! Before you know it, you'll get a private e-mail back from a teacher with helpful advice on where to find the answer to your question!

☛ **IMPORTANT!** When you send your question using the teacher pager, make sure you ask specific questions. If you just say, "I don't understand my math homework," no one will know what you're talking about. But if you say, "I don't understand the Pythagorean theorem," the teacher will be able to help you.

A word of warning: If you're hoping the online teachers will simply do your homework for you, forget it. Their job is to help you, not to do it for you. They'll encourage you and point you in the right direction, but it's still up to you to do the work. Just like teachers! Too bad, huh?

LIVE CHAT! AAC'S HAL ROSENGARTEN - - - - -

Henry "Hal" Rosengarten runs the Academic Assistance Center on America Online. He has been teaching sixth grade in the Marlboro, New York, middle school for nearly thirty years. A dedicated teacher, Hal is always working with kids, either in class or in his "seventy-hour-a-week part-time job" as AAC coordinator.

Pondiscio: Tell me about AAC, Hal. How did it get started?

Rosengarten: Mark Hulme, an elementary school teacher in Georgia and an AOL user since 1988, came up with the idea. The Interactive Educational Services, IES, was created in 1989 and he was the first coordinator. They offered online classes (for a fee) and a live tutoring room. I joined in 1993, and the IES and AAC separated in early 1994. Since then we've grown from 1 room, 130 teachers, and perhaps 10,000 users a month to 5 rooms, nearly 1,000 teachers, and 150,000 students a month. In addition, we brought the teacher pager service from 10 questions a day to over 4,000 and from 1 topic to 9. Now, with the release of the Knowledge Database we see only a few more things we want to add, but as technology improves so will our service.

Pondiscio: Are all the teachers who offer online help to students real-life teachers like you?

Rosengarten: No. We have about twenty lawyers, probably nearly the same amount of doctors, maybe thirty to forty nurses, accountants, engineers, politicians, one professional athlete, an auto mechanic, etc. We try to hire based on the types of questions the kids ask. Of about six hundred actual teachers, perhaps one hundred are retired, disabled, or out for child-care leave.

Pondiscio: How do you find all those volunteers to help kids with their homework?

Rosengarten: They come to us. Most of them are people who stumbled on to the room or whose children or students have used it. In addition, we have received considerable publicity, and people come looking for us. In a few areas—math, science, and history—we have actually placed want ads in various places online and have asked our staff and students to seek more teachers. I would like to have twelve hundred to fifteen hundred teachers on the staff soon.

Pondiscio: How do you handle all those teacher pager questions?

Rosengarten: Until early 1994 it worked fine. Send your question in, and one of our trained staff members would distribute it to several experts in that field. You would then get a reply, sometimes within an hour, sometimes the following day, by e-mail. But then we became popular. By May 1995 we were receiving several hundred questions a day. Now we receive several *thousand* pager questions a day, with over sixty people distributing the questions to our experts twenty-four hours a day.

Pondiscio: Is the teacher pager the most popular part of AAC?

Rosengarten: The rooms and the pager are very popular, followed by our twenty-eight message boards and contests. But we hope that the Knowledge Database will surpass them all.

Pondiscio: How did you personally get involved in online education, Hal?

Rosengarten: I joined as a teacher. I had taught sixth grade for twenty-five years and wanted to expand my outlook. I was growing stale.

Pondiscio: Is there a big difference between teaching in the class and teaching online?

Rosengarten: It's totally different. You really do not know anything about the kids you are teaching online—in fact, sometimes we are not even sure if we are helping a kid or an adult! The kids also have a tendency to test the teachers—we get a lot of kids acting up, far more than we would in a class. Since they think we can't contact their parents, they misbehave and sometimes disrupt the room. But we have a full-time person who watches for such things and sends them to the master account, so that problem does not last for long.

Pondiscio: Is that the biggest difference?

Rosengarten: The most important thing, as far as teaching is concerned, is that the kids are not afraid or shy. Many of the kids who would never raise their hands in class are very verbal online. They are not visible—no one can hear their voice or see what they are wearing. Three of my own students use the AAC quite a bit, even though they know who I am. They are very shy in class, would not ask for extra help, but when they get home they contact me.

EXTRA HELP ON THE WEB

The Academic Assistance Center on AOL may be the only place online where you can interact in a live, real-time chat with a tutor, but there are plenty of places on the Web where you can get extra help one-on-one.

INTERNET PUBLIC LIBRARY
(http://ipl.sils.umich.edu/)
Just like a real library, the University of Michigan's Internet public library has different sections and rooms you can wander in and out of looking for help. It's a must-see Web site, complete with a giant electronic card catalogue of reference works, with a Youth section featuring a librarian who is game to help tackle homework questions, a Teen section for older kids, links to all the best search engines on the Web, an exhibit hall—everything but a warm, comfy couch to curl up on with a book!

DIAL-A-TEACHER ONLINE
(http://tiger.chuh.cleveland-heights.k12.oh.us/
DAT/DAT.html)
This is an online version of Cleveland Heights Teachers Union Dial-a-Teacher telephone service. If you're having trouble with your homework or need suggestions on how to improve your study habits, check it out.

ASK THE EXPERTS

There's a Woody Allen movie in which two guys are standing in line at a movie theater arguing about the theories of sixties media guru Marshall McLuhan. One of them says, "Well I happen to have Marshall McLuhan right here." The professor walks over and says, "He's right. You don't understand my work at all."

Wouldn't it be great if you could prove a point that way?

E-mail makes that possible. Well, you can't send e-mail to Marshall McLuhan, because he's dead. But you can use the Net as a way to get information from people all over the world, including experts in dozens of fields.

Here are a few sites specifically designed for finding expert help:

ALCOM Ask a Scientist
   (http://alcom.kent.edu/ALCOM/K12/ASK/
   Ask_feedback.html)

Ask a Doc (http://www.rain.org/~medmall/
   askadoc.htm)

Ask a Librarian (Indiana University)
(http://www.iusb.edu/webacts/libg/Ask.html)

Ask a Physicist (http://twsuvm.uc.twsu.edu/
~obswww/)

Ask a Question on Judaism
(http://www.chabad.org/question.htm)

Ask an Animal Keeper (Micke Grove Zoo)
(http://www.inreach.com/mgzoo/pages/
aska.htm)

Ask an Astronomer (http://twsuvm.uc.twsu.edu/
~obswww/)

Ask an Expert (http://www.usa.net/~pitsco/
pitsco/ask.html)

Ask an Expert Page—with links to many others
(http://njnie.dl.stevens-tech.edu/curriculum/
ask.html)

Ask Dr. Math (http://forum.swarthmore.edu/
dr.math/)

Ask Dr. Neutrino (physics)
(http://nike.phy.bris.ac.uk/dr/ask.html)

Ask the Amish! (http://padutch.welcome.com/
askamish.html)

Ask the Author/Internet Public Library
(http://ipl.sils.umich.edu/youth/AskAuthor/
authorinfo.html)

Ask the Classics Expert (UCLA)
(http://www.humnet.ucla.edu/humnet/classics/
questions.html)

Ask the Engineer (Intel)
(http://www.intel.com/intel/educate/kids/
askeng.html)

NASA: Ask the Astronomers
(http://umbra.nascom.nasa.gov/spartan/
ask_astronomers.htm)

Professor's Door Is Open
(http://he.tdl.com/~silicons/net1prof.htm)

The Young Scientist Program (Ask-a-Scientist)
(http://medinfo.wustl.edu/~ysp)

U.S. Geological Survey Ask-a-Geologist (earth
science)
(http://walrus.wr.usgs.gov/docs/ask-a-ge.html)

ONLINE PEOPLE

Sometimes the most interesting and useful sources of
information available online are the people you meet
in cyberspace. If you're looking for advanced help—
or you want to spice up a report with an authoritative quote from an expert in the subject you're studying—you can get the answers you need with just a
little extra effort. Learning from people online is also
a great way to put classroom lessons to work in the
real world:

- Students in Mary Meewes's math class at Oviedo
  High School in Florida go online to learn about
  the practical ways in which math is used by people in the real world. They recently wrote letters
  asking about the importance of math in nonscien-
  tific fields and heard from engineers, government
  workers, and office managers about how they use
  math in their jobs every day. As a result, it's been
  a long time since anyone in class asked, "What
  do I need to know this stuff for anyway?"

- "I was doing a report on repressed memory and

119

I used AOL to get magazine articles of cases and theories," says Becky Schile, who attends Petaluma High School in California. "I posted a note in Compton's Study Break because I was looking for someone to interview that had experienced repressed memory to make my paper stronger. I was lucky and someone e-mailed me who was willing to help."

- Joan Berger's fifth grade classes at East Hills School in Roslyn, New York, conduct lots of online interviews with computer experts, astronomers, marine biologists, undercover narcotics agents, scientists, and lots of other experts throughout the school year.

- Kansas City high school student Tiffinie Gary has a unique strategy for getting extra help online: "I ask my teachers if they use America Online, and if they say yes, then I ask them what their screen names are. Asking questions online is less embarrassing to most kids than actually asking a 'stupid' question right in the middle of class."

Throughout this book, we've mentioned places on the commercial online services and the Web where people with interests and expertise in many different subjects gather (see Chapter Six, "Subject by Subject"). These are great places to look for experts in the subjects you're studying. And don't forget Usenet newsgroups and mailing lists (see Chapter Four, "Searching the Internet"). Bulletin boards on the commercial online services are also excellent places to look. Ask around in discussion groups. You'll be surprised how easy it is to track down people who know a lot about a subject—no matter what the subject is!

And it's not just the experts who can make the difference between a passing grade and an *A*. With a little imagination, you can find someone online who can add a little something extra to an ordinary report. AOL member Joellen Schneider had to do a report on Algeria recently. "I used the reference section for the encyclopedia and to get general information. I also got names of books written by people from Algeria," she said. "But the greatest advantage AOL gave me was that I used the member directory to find someone who was Algerian. The girl I talked to gave me a lot of information because she had lived in Algeria for most of her life. She was going to college in the United States. I interviewed her, and she even sent me items from Algeria to use in my presentation. I got an *A+* on my report."

IMPROVE YOUR STUDY SKILLS ONLINE -

Do you spend too much time studying? Not enough? Do you get tired easily? Do you do homework with the TV or radio turned on? Do you write your papers the night before they're due? If you need to develop better study habits, there are lots of places online to turn for help. Check out some of these sites:

Academic Skills Center
   (http://coos.dartmouth.edu/~gmz/asctr.html)

Study Skills Self-help Information
   (http://www.ucc.vt.edu/stdysk/stdyhlp.html)

- -

BE AN EXPERT!

The Internet community works best when people co-operate—giving back something for all the information they've received. If you expect others to help you online, you should try to help others in return. For fourth graders at Wilder Elementary School, Mansfield, Missouri, that means being the experts for other kids. Their hometown is also the hometown of Laura Ingalls Wilder, the author of *Little House on the Prarie* and the other "Little House" books. They go on the Net to answer questions about the author from other kids reading her books.

You can go online to get extra help from other students, too. If you're learning Spanish, French, German, or some other language, try finding an online key pal in another country to practice with. If you find students who are learning English, that gives *you* the chance to be the expert!

Museums and More in Cyberspace

"The Internet rules! We can use it for talking to people all over the world. I have learned a lot of stuff about the States. I liked finding pictures of Yosemite."

—BRIANNA, grade 5
Bass Lake Elementary School
Bass Lake, CA

The word *museum* comes from the ancient Greek word *Mouseion*, "of the houses," the nine goddesses in Greek mythology who presided over the arts and sciences. Most people now think of museums as places where works of art and other important objects are stored and displayed. With that definition, you're going to have to start calling your computer a museum, because it can display thousands of works of art and cool exhibits for you.

In fact, you no longer need a passport and an airline ticket to visit the best museums, libraries, zoos, and attractions. Many of the greatest cultural institutions in the world now come to *you* via modem. Virtual art museums make it possible to view Picassos, van Goghs, and Renoirs on your computer screen. Online multimedia exhibits from NASA and the Smithsonian Institution introduce you to a mind-boggling collection of science and historical data. The Library of Congress and dozens of universities offer electronic galleries with everything from rare books and manuscripts to photographs ready for downloading. This chapter will point you to some of the best online museums and other online hot spots and what you can find there.

MEGAMUSEUMS

SMITHSONIAN ONLINE
(http://www.si.edu)
The Smithsonian Institution in Washington, D.C., has been called "the nation's attic." It's not a single museum but a collection of museums, including the National Museum of American History, the National Air and Space Museum, the National Museum of African Art, the National Museum of Natural History, and many others, all represented online. That makes Smithsonian Online on the Web and on AOL (key words: Smithsonian, Si) a terrific place to see exhibits on dozens of topics. You can do a simple key-word search to turn up information on almost any subject from the museums' collections, or browse through photographs and articles from *Smithsonian* magazine.

LIBRARY OF CONGRESS
(http://lcweb.loc.gov/)

Want to see the original Declaration of Independence, the Gettysburg Address, or the only known photograph of President Abraham Lincoln giving the speech? You can see many famous documents from U.S. history at the Library of Congress Web site. In addition to its massive storehouse of information, the Library of Congress's Web Site features a regular schedule of online exhibits on a wide variety of topics, including women journalists during World War II; the building of Washington, D.C.; African-American culture and history; Columbus's voyage to the New World; the Dead Sea scrolls; and many more! The American Memory section lets you listen to audio recordings of the country's leaders. An amazing online resource!

THE NATIONAL ARCHIVES
(http://www.nara.gov/)

If the Smithsonian Institution is the nation's attic, then the National Archives and Records Administration (NARA) is its secretary. NARA is responsible for keeping the records of the federal government. They've inaugurated a new exhibit hall on the World Wide Web where Internet users will be able to access selected items from the National Archives holdings. Recent exhibits have focused on the Declaration of Independence, the Constitution, and the Bill of Rights. There's always a featured document on display, like the Emancipation Proclamation. Other recent exhibits have been "Poster Art from World War II" and "A Day in the Life of the President."

NATURAL HISTORY MUSEUMS

THE FIELD MUSEUM OF NATURAL HISTORY
(http://www.bvis.uic.edu/museum/)
The Field Museum of Natural History in Chicago is dinosaur headquarters on the Web! Click on the Exhibitions button to find out what life was like before, during, and after dinosaurs. And don't miss the neat exhibition on bats and the grimacing masks from the island of Java.

THE NATURAL HISTORY MUSEUM, LONDON
(http://www.nhm.ac.uk/)
London's Natural History Museum was the first British national museum to have a Web site. This site is divided into four main sections. The first section, The Museum, offers an online version of current exhibitions at the museum, as well as special online-only exhibitions. There's also a Discovery Centre (don't you love the way the British spell?) just for kids. Click on the Science area to see home pages on botany, zoology, entomology, mineralogy, and paleontology—some of which may be beyond all but the most advanced students. "Information" gives access to the museum's libraries and a number of the museum's databases.

CLEVELAND MUSEUM OF NATURAL HISTORY
(http://www.cmnh.org)
This site is so much fun, you'll forget it's a museum. The Cleveland Museum of Natural History lets you uncover the roots of your family tree, starting with "Lucy," the extraordinary three-million-year-old woman—all seventy pounds of her! Visit the shaggy-

haired mastodons and saber-toothed cats of the Ice Age. Or go back even further to when colossal dinosaurs roamed the earth. Uncover the earth, one layer at a time. Learn all about earth-shattering quakes and erupting volcanos. Investigate the dark mysteries of a natural cavern. Check out the earth's harvest of minerals and gemstones. Learn about societies living in harmony with nature and travel the seven continents without ever packing a suitcase. A terrific site!

THE ROYAL BRITISH COLUMBIA MUSEUM
(http://rbcm1.rbcm.gov.bc.ca/)
One of the world's leading museums offers one of the best museum Web sites. It's largely dedicated to the natural history of the area around Victoria in British Columbia, Canada, but there's a lot to interest virtual visitors from everywhere. See a woolly mammoth, which roamed Canada as recently as nine thousand years ago. Check out pictures of Ice Age mammals, some of which are extinct, others of which survive to this day. The First Nations' exhibit offers a glimpse at the lives of North America's earliest settlers, thousands of years ago.

UNIVERSITY OF CALIFORNIA MUSEUM OF PALEONTOLOGY
(http://ucmp1.berkeley.edu/)
Check out animal, vegetable, and mineral fossils from millons of years ago or just go directly to the hall of dinosaurs and roam among raptors, stegosaurs, *T. rex*, and more! And when you're done roaming the exhibits, hop on the museum's "subway" system, which has hundreds of links to other great museums and science sites!

A WORLD OF NATURAL HISTORY MUSEUMS

Academy of Natural Sciences of Philadelphia
(http://www.acnatsci.org/)

Burke Museum, University of Washington, Seattle
(http://weber.u.washington.edu/~burkemus/)

The California Academy of Sciences
(http://www.calacademy.org/)

Chicago Academy of Sciences Nature Museum
(http://www.chias.org/)

The Electronic Prehistoric Shark Museum
(http://turnpike.net/emporium/C/celestial/
epsm.htm)

Fernbank Museum of Natural History, Atlanta,
Georgia
(http://stlbbg.gtri.gatech.edu/)

Finnish Museum of Natural History: Botanical
Museum
(http://www.helsinki.fi/kmus/)

The Florida Museum of Natural History
(http://www.flmnh.ufl.edu/)

Honolulu Community College Dinosaur Exhibit
(http://www.hcc.hawaii.edu/dinos/dinos.1.html)

Illinois State Museum
(http://www.museum.state.il.us/)

Kansas University Natural History Museum
(http://ukanaix.cc.ukans.edu/~kanu/)

Manchester Museum
(http://www.mcc.ac.uk/~mellorir/museum.html)

Museum of Jurassic Technology
(http://www.mjt.org/)

National Dinosaur Museum, Gungaughlin, Australia
(http://www.world.net/Travel/Australia/dino-museum)

Natural History Museum of Los Angeles County
(http://www.lam.mus.ca.us/lacmnh)

Natural History Web
(http://nmnhgoph.si.edu/nmnhweb.html)

The New Mexico Museum of Natural History and Science
(http://www.aps.edu/HTMLPages/NMMNH.html)

North Carolina Museum of Life and Science
(http://ils.unc.edu/NCMLS/ncmls.html)

Nova Scotia Museum
(http://www.ednet.ns.ca/edu/museum/)

The Royal Tyrrell Museum of Paleontology
(http://www.tyrrell.com/welcome.html)

The Smithsonian Institution, National Museum of Natural History
(http://nmnhwww.si.edu)

The Swedish Museum of Natural History
(http://www.nrm.se/)

University of Georgia Museum of Natural History
(http://gis.lislab.uga.edu/natmus)

University of Michigan Exhibit Museum of Natural History
(http://www.exhibits.lsa.umich.edu/)

Wayne State Fossil Museum
(http://gopher.science.wayne.edu/animals/fossil/index.html)

ART MUSEUMS

NATIONAL MUSEUM OF AMERICAN ART
(http://www.mnaa.si.edu)
The National Museum of American Art is yet another part of the Smithsonian Institution. You can visit on the Web or on AOL (key words: NMAA, American art). Almost one thousand works of art are on display at their Web site, from the permanent collection as well as current exhibitions. And it's all fully searchable! If you're looking for a specific painter's work, just type in the name and hit Search. All the works of art in the collection by that artist pop up with a thumbnail picture of the paintings. Click on a picture and it fills your screen. And there's plenty of biographical data about the painter and easy-to-understand art history info.

You can browse art reference resources, bibliographies, artists' photos, and publications; talk about art and art issues with other aficionados and NMAA staff; enter art contests; even upload your own works for aesthetic evaluation by a Smithsonian curator! There's a special section of activities for teachers and kids. This is an online art museum as it should be!

WEBMUSEUM, PARIS
(http://sunsite.unc.edu/wm/)
The WebMuseum, Paris, is a legendary art site, and for good reason. It's well organized, easy to use, and bursting with some of the most famous paintings in the world. Art students will love the glossary of painting styles, which offers simple descriptions of every school of art from Baroque to Cubism to Impressionism to Surrealism. Don't miss it! And while you're there, take the virtual tour of Paris.

WORLD WIDE ARTS RESOURCES
(http://www.concourse.com/wwar)

This site isn't a museum itself, but if you're an art lover, it's still a must-see. It offers hypertext links to more than 250 museums worldwide, over 500 galleries and exhibitions, and dozens of art publications and arts-related institutions. There's also an index of major artists and lots more—the most comprehensive arts source on the Web!

MORE ART MUSEUMS

Asian Art Museum of San Francisco
(http://sfasian.apple.com/)

Banff Centre for the Arts
(http://www.banffcentre.ab.ca/)

The Brooklyn Museum
(http://wwar.com/brooklyn_museum/index.html)

Butler Institute of American Art
(http://www.butlerart.com/)

Michael C. Carlos Museum/Emory University
(http://www.cc.emory.edu/CARLOS)

Leonardo da Vinci Museum
(http://cellini.leonardo.net/museum)

DaliWeb
(http://www.highwayone.com/dali)

Dallas Museum of Art
(http://www.unt.edu/dfw/dma/www/dma.htm)

George Eastman House—Museum of Photography
(http://www.it.rit.edu:80/~gehouse/)

Fine Arts Museums of San Francisco
(http://www.island.cmo/famsf/)

Glenbow Museum
(http://www.lexicom.ab.ca/~glenbow/)

The High Museum of Art
(http://isotropic.com/highmuse/
highhome.html#homepage)

KOMA: Korean Museum of Art and Cultural Center
(http://anet.net.koma/)

The Krannert Art Museum
(http://www.art.uiuc.edu/kam/)

Los Angeles County Museum of Art
(http://www.lacma.org/)

Minneapolis Institute of Arts
(http://www.mtn.org/MIA/)

Montreal Museum of Art
(http://www.interax.net/tcenter/tour/mba.
html)

Musée du Louvre
(http://www.paris.org.:80/Musees/Louvre/)

The Museum of Modern Art, New York
(http://www.sva.edu/moma/)

National Gallery of Canada
(http://national.gallery.ca/serve3.htm)

National Portrait Gallery
(http://www.si.edu/organiza/)

Palmer Museum of Art
(http://cac.psu.edu/~mtd120/palmer/)

Philadelphia Museum of Art
(http://www.libertynet.org:80/~pma/)

UNC Virtual Museum
  (http://sunsite.unc.edu/exhibits/vmuseum/)

The Andy Warhol Museum
  (http://www.warhol.org/warhol/warhol.html)

Whitney Museum of American Art
  (http://mosaic.echonyc.com/~whitney)

HISTORICAL AND CULTURAL TREASURES

THE NATIONAL MUSEUM OF AMERICAN HISTORY
(http://www.si.edu/organiza/museums/nmah/homepage/gallery.htm)
Take a tour through our nation's history—from the Revolutionary War to today's technology revolution—by exploring all three floors of the Smithsonian's Museum of American History. On the first floor, look at the first railroads in the United States; on the second floor, see all the presidents' wives in the First Ladies gallery; on the third floor, tinker with technology!

PRESIDENT
(http://sunsite.unc.edu/lia/president/)
Looking for information about the life and times of the presidents of the United States of America (the guys who live in the White House, not the band)? Every president since Herbert Hoover has a presidential library built in their honor, usually in their hometown, to store all their important papers and memorabilia. The Presidential Library System has established this central home page, called President, with links to all eleven presidential libraries.

THE INDIAN PUEBLO CULTURAL CENTER
(http://hanksville.phast.umass.edu/defs/
independent/PCC/PCC.html#toc)
Do you know which Native American tribes live in
New Mexico? Do you know why some tribes are
called Pueblo? Find out by visiting this site and
learning more about their lives, their art, and their
homes.

UNIVERSITY OF MEMPHIS INSTITUTE OF
EGYPTIAN ART AND ARCHAEOLOGY
(http://www.memphis.edu/egypt/main.html)
At the University of Memphis Institute of Egyptian
Art and Archaeology's Web site, you not only get to
visit a two-thousand-year-old mummy named Iret-
iruw (pronounced "ear-et ear-oo"), but you can also
look at special statues and objects that people in ancient Egypt buried with their dead—including a four-
thousand-year-old piece of bread! You can also look
at a color slide show all about Egypt.

MORE HISTORY AND CULTURAL MUSEUMS

Chesapeake Bay Maritime Museum
   (http://www.washcoll.edu/museum/bay.html)

Chicago Historical Society
   (http://www.chicagohs.org)

Golden Gate Railroad Museum
   (http://www.io.com/~fano2472/ggrm)

Henry Ford Museum & Greenfield Village
   (http://hfm.umd.umich.edu)

Jewish Museum, New York
   (http://www.jtsa.edu/jm/index.html)

Mariners' Museum, Newport News, Virginia
(http://www.mariner.org/mariner)

Museum of American Frontier Culture
(http://www.elpress.com/staunton/
FNTRCLT.HTML)

Museum of American Political Life
(http://www.hartford.edu/polmus/
polmus1.html)

Museum of Slavery in the Atlantic
(http://squash.la.psu.edu/plarson/smuseum/
homepage.html)

Mystic Seaport Museum
(http://www.mystic.org)

National Civil Rights Museum
(http://www.magibox.net:80/~ncrm)

Old Sturbridge Village Museum
(http://www.osv.org)

Oriental Institute Museum, Chicago
(http://www-oi.uchicago.edu/OI/MUS/
OI_Museum.html)

The Papers of George Washington
(http://poe.acc.Virginia.edu/~gwpapers/
GWhome.html)

Union Pacific Museum
(http://www.infoanalytic.com/upmuseum/)

United States Holocaust Memorial Museum
(http://www.ushmm.org/)

SCIENCE MUSEUMS

THE EXPLORATORIUM
(http://www.exploratorium.edu/)
Kids in San Francisco know that the Exploratorium is one of the coolest hands-on science museums around. Now you can explore their virtual exhibitions online. Learn why your eyes sometimes see shapes, colors, and textures that aren't there—and why you have more in common with fruit flies than you might think.

THE NATIONAL AIR AND SPACE MUSEUM
(http://www.nasm.edu/NASMpage.html)
One of the most popular science museums in the country is now online. Click on Galleries to wander through the museum's permanent exhibitions: "Apollo to the Moon," "Pioneers in Flight," "World War II Aviation," and more. Click on the hypertext links, and photos of the Wright brothers' 1903 flyer, Lindbergh's *Spirit of St. Louis,* and the *Apollo 11* command module appears on your screen. Or go to the museum's **Center for Earth and Planetary Studies** (http://ceps.nasm.edu:2020/), where you can look at photographs that the space shuttle has taken of earth's volcanoes, oceans, and mountains from outer space. There's lots to see here!

THE FRANKLIN INSTITUTE SCIENCE MUSEUM
(http://sln.fi.edu/tfi/welcome.html)
You may know that Benjamin Franklin was one of the Founding Fathers of the United States, but did you know that he was also a scientist who performed pioneering experiments with electricity? Learn all

about Ben, for whom this Philadelphia-based museum is named, and all the neat things he discovered and invented. Beyond Ben, take an inside-and-out tour of the human heart—including pictures and movies of real-life human hearts at work!

LOS ALAMOS NATIONAL LABORATORY
(http://128.165.1.1/solarsys/)
Los Alamos National Laboratory, a scientific research center in New Mexico, has complied an eye-popping collection of full-color photos on our solar system's planets, and tons of interesting and fun facts about them: statistics about their size, mass, features, distance from the sun and the earth, and a lot more.

SCIENCE MUSEUM OF MINNESOTA "MAYA ADVENTURE"
(http://ties.k12.mn.us/~smm/)
Did you know that the Mayans lived in Mexico even before Mexicans? Learn all about the Mayans, check out the ancient pyramids where their ancestors lived, their homes today, the crafts they make, and try your hand at some neat activities!

MORE SCIENCE MUSEUMS

The Art of Renaissance Science
(http://www.cuny.edu/multimedia/arsnew/arstitle.html)

Boston Museum of Science
(http://www.mos.org/)

Carnegie Science Center
(http://www.csc.clpgh.org/)

Explorit Science Center (Davis, California)
(http://198.215.124.201/fwmsh.html)

Fort Worth Museum of Science and History
(http://198.215.124.201/fwmsh.html)

History of Science Museum in Florence, Italy
(http://galileo.imss.firenze.it/index.html)

Miami Museum of Science
(http://www.miamisci.org/)

National Museum of Science and Technology
(Ottawa, Ontario, Canada)
(http://www.digimark.net/iatech)

New England Science Center
(http://www.nesc.org/)

Oregon Museum of Science and Industry
(http://www.omsi.edu/)

Science Museum of Virginia
(http://smv.mus.va.us)

Science World (Vancouver, British Columbia,
Canada)
(http://www.scienceworld.bc.ca/)

The Sciencenter (Ithaca, New York)
(http://edison.scictr.cornell.edu/)

SciTech Science and Technology Interactive Center
(http://town.hall.org/places/SciTech/)

St. Louis Science Center
(http://www.slsc.org/)

WWW Virtual Library: History of Science
(http://www.asap.unimelb.edu.au/hstm/
hstm_ove.htm)

OBSERVATORIES

NASA SPACE TELESCOPE SCIENCE INSTITUTE
(http://stsci.edu/pubinfo/BestOfHST95.html)
Get a close-up, full-color view of our solar system
with photographs of the universe taken by the Hubble Space Telescope. You can look at stars and super-
novas, plus animations of comet Shoemaker-Levy
colliding with Jupiter!

MOUNT WILSON OBSERVATORY
(http://www.mtwilson.edu/)
Go to tourist information and take a "walking" tour
through most of the observatory and then through
the observatory grounds. There is a customized star
map, a constellation quiz, information on the history
of the observatory and scientific programs at the
observatory.

MORE OBSERVATORIES

Big Bear Solar Observatory
(http://sundog.caltech.edu/)

The Burke-Gaffney Observatory
(http://apwww.stmarys.ca/bgo/html)

Griffith Observatory
(http://www.csun.edu/~hbphy003/)

Lowell Observatory Home Page
(http://www.lowell.edu/)

McDonald Observatory
(http://www.as.utexas.edu/PIO/PIO_page.html)

Mount Laguna Observatory
(http://mintaka.sdsu.edu/)

Mount Washington Observatory
(http://www.mountwashington.org/)

National Undergraduate Research Observatory
(http://nuro.phy.nau.edu/)

Palomar Observatory
(http://astro.caltech.edu/observatories/palomar/)

South Pole Observatory
(http://www.cmdl.noaa.gov/spo/spo.html)

ZOOS, AQUARIA, AND BOTANIC GARDENS

ZOONET
(http://www.mindspring.com/~zoonet/)
Created in late 1994, ZooNet is simply an attempt to provide a single point of entry to all zoos, everywhere in the world. Webmaster Jim Henley says, "as a father, educator and Net surfer I saw a need to aid parents and educators in helping them locate information for their children and students on the World Wide Web; in my case I zeroed in on zoos." Not only does ZooNet provide the most comprehensive collection of links to other zoos anywhere, it also has the best collection of animal pictures on the Web.

NATIONAL ZOOLOGICAL PARK HOME PAGE
(http://www.si.edu/organiza/museums/zoo)
The National Zoo, in Wasington, D.C., doesn't see itself as a zoo, but rather a BioPark—part wildlife, natural history museum, botanic garden, aquarium, and even art gallery. Zoo, BioPark, whatever . . . there's plenty to see for the animal lover, including a great library of animal photos and educational games. A first-rate site!

MORE ZOOS TO VISIT

Austin Zoo
(http://www.onr.com/austinzoo/)

Birmingham Zoo
(http://www.bhm.tis.net/zoo)

Cincinnati Zoo & Botanical Garden
(http://www.cincyzoo.org/)

Florida Aquarium
(http://www.sptimes.com/aquarium/
default.html)

Great Barrier Reef Aquarium
(http://aquarium.gbrmpa.gov.au/)

Hall of Mammals
(http://ucmp1.berkeley.edu/exhibittext/
mammal.html)

Monterey Bay Aquarium
(http://www.usw.nps.navy.mil/~millercw/aq/)

New England Aquarium
(http://www.neaq.org/)

Phoenix Zoo Home Page
(http://aztec.asu.edu/phxzoo/homepage.html)

San Diego Zoo
(http://www.sandiegozoo.org)

San Francisco Aquarium Society
(http://members.aol.com/sfas/)

Seattle Aquarium
(http://www.speakeasy.org/aquarium/)

Tennessee Aquarium Home Page
(http://www.tennis.org/)

University of Delaware—Botanic Garden
(http://bluehen.ags.udel.edu/udgarden.html)

Woodland Park Zoo
  (http://www.zoo.org/)

NEITHER FISH NOR FOWL

NATIONAL MUSEUM OF THE AMERICAN INDIAN
(http://www.si.edu/nmai/)

Not every online museum is part of the Smithsonian Institution. But many of the best ones are, including this site devoted to one of the Smithsonian's newest museums. The museum's mission is to preserve "the life, languages, literature, history, and arts of Native Americans." A great site to visit when your social studies class is learning about America's first people.

GREAT OUTDOOR RECREATION PAGE
(http://www.gorp.com/gorp/resource/main.htm)

Great Outdoor Recreation Page (GORP) has links leading to national parks, forests, wilderness areas, wildlife refuges, monuments, archaeological and paleontological sites, historic parks, recreation areas, seashores, primitive areas, scenic areas, memorials, battlefields, and marine sanctuary programs. "The United States's National Parks contain some of the most beautiful and extraordinary natural wonders in the country," notes this site. Unfortunately, you can't see them on this text-only Web site. It's still a good resource—especially for planning trips to the hundreds of locations listed.

MUSEUM OF THE CITY OF SAN FRANCISCO
(http://www.slip.net/~dfowler/1906/06.html)

This site contains lots of information on the 1906 earthquake, including a map of the epicenter, reports from the fire and police departments, eyewitness accounts, scientific reports, relief and recovery efforts, and photographs.

MORE MUSEUMS

California Surf Museum
  (http://www.surfart.com/casmhmpg.htm)

Firehouse Museum
  (http://www.globalinfo.com/noncomm/
  firehouse/Firehouse.html)

The American Museum of Fly Fishing
  (http://www.gorp.com/cl_angle/canecoun/
  museum.htm)

The Computer Museum Network
  (http://www.net.org/)

The International Horse Museum Online
  (http://www.horseworld.com/imh/
  imhmain.html)

The Internet Museum of Holography
  (http://www.enter.net/~holostudio/edu.html)

WHAT? YOU WANT MORE??!?

**The World Wide Virtual Library: Museums
(http://www.comlab.ox.ac.uk/archive/other/
museums.html)**
There are literally thousands of online museums and libraries—nobody knows exactly how many—and more come online all the time. If you haven't seen anything to grab your interest among the dozens

listed in this chapter, check your pulse, then point your Web browser to the World Wide Virtual Library. They are constantly surfing the Web looking for new and interesting online exhibits.

A+ Projects You Can Do Online

"Going online definitely makes my schoolwork and projects much easier and much more fun than spending an hour at the library."

—RAE KAPLAN

You don't need a computer and a modem to do your homework. But having one can be the difference between making homework a boring chore or fun. With a little imagination, and knowing what to do, you can use your computer and modem to express your creativity (and impress your teachers).

Here are just a few ideas for online projects.

- For a report on the Great Depression or World War II, log on to SeniorNet on AOL (key word: Senior) or the Web and find someone who lived through those days to interview about their experiences.

- How are the day-to-day lives of students in your

school similar and different from the lives of kids in other parts of the country and the world? Chronicle a day in your life and trade your story with kids in other cities and countries.

- Learning about earthquakes? Go to Mercury Center on AOL (key word: Mercury), the online service of the *San Jose Mercury-News*. Look in the message boards for someone to interview who lived through the big San Francisco earthquake in 1989.

- Study the holidays and customs of other countries and cultures by writing to key pals in other countries about the holidays they recognize and how they celebrate them.

- Go online to survey kids in other cities about issues in the news; the cost of food, clothing, and other necessities—or just fun things like favorite music, movies, and TV shows.

Kerry McCaughan, a seventh grader at Lost Mountain Middle School in Kennesaw, Georgia, describes a recent science project she and her classmates did online. "In science, our class gathers water from rain gauges we have set outside our school, and we test it to see if it is acidic or not, using pH paper. We send our results to other schools who are also in the project all over the country and the world. And they send us their results also. The head of the program is involved with the Environmental Protection Agency, and she shows them our results. By getting involved in this, our class gets to learn about testing rainwater and how our everyday life affects the environment in which we live, and also how to get a link to other schools and find friends using the World

Wide Web. It is all very interesting, and the whole class is excited about it!"

RESOURCES FOR ONLINE PROJECTS

Looking for ideas for online projects? Looking for partners to work with? Either way, here are some great places to start.

KIDLINK
(http://www.kidlink.org/)
Kidlink is a grassroots project based in Norway that gets kids ages ten to fifteen involved in a global dialogue with one another. Since its start in 1990, over fifty thousand kids from eighty countries on all continents have participated in Kidlink activities, like key pals, educational projects, live chats, and more. Kidlink has several different forums for youth dialogue—both for individuals and classrooms. All Kidlink youth participants begin by responding to four questions:

Who am I?
What do I want to be when I grow up?
How do I want the world to be better when I grow up?
What can I do now to make this happen?

After you have introduced yourself by answering these four questions, you can participate in any of the Kidlink projects.

You can also participate in Kidlink via e-mail. Just write to LISTSERV@VM1.NODAK.EDU. In the message body, type: subscribe kidlink [your name].

You'll be chatting with other kids from all over the world in no time!

I*EARN
One of the most ambitious networks to connect kids for school projects all over the world is the International Education and Resource Network (I*EARN). It links teachers and students in over one thousand schools in dozens of countries all over the world, including the United States, Russia, China, Israel, Australia, Japan, and Kenya. Online I*EARN student projects give students the opportunity to learn about other cultures and work with kids all over the world on school projects. To learn more, send e-mail to: iearn@copenfund.igc.apc.org.

THE ELECTRONIC SCHOOLHOUSE
The Electronic Schoolhouse on American Online (key word: ESH) is a place where entire classes, teachers, and individual students can meet to work on projects together. ESH also runs lots of their own projects. Some of the areas offered include the "Schoolhouse" for live class-to-class connections with up to twenty-two other schools at the same time. The Student-to-Student message board is where you'll find other kids hard at work and play. ESH's best-known project is the ScrapBook Writing Project, in which kids share stories about where they live and go to school. Others include Geography Detectives, where classes are paired and mail each other boxes containing clues to where they live; and the Online Academic Bowl, where students write the questions and join with other schools for live quiz shows online.

GLOBAL SCHOOLHOUSE
(http://www.gsh.org)

The Global Schoolhouse is a project of the Global SchoolNet Foundation, funded in part by the National Science Foundation and supported by many local and national businesses. It connects schools and students nationally and internationally over the Internet. Kids do collaborative research and use video-conferencing to communicate with one another and national and international leaders, including U.S. Senators, Dr. C. Everett Koop, and anthropologist Dr. Jane Goodall. If your school is not up to speed on computers and the Internet, tell your teacher about the Global SchoolNet Foundation's teacher workshops, including "Hello Internet," which introduces teachers to Internet resources useful in the classroom.

ACADEMY ONE
(http://www.nptn.org/cyber.serv/AOneP/)

Academy One is part of the National Public Telecomputing Network (NPTN), which is to the online world what public TV and National Public Radio are to broadcasting. Academy One is an online resource for teachers, students, parents, and administrators from kindergarten through high school. Academy One organizes online projects that let students share their creative writing, artwork, science experiments, or research results with other students via computer. Students can also exchange messages with schools in foreign countries or in foreign languages, and share their involvement in projects that help their communities or address social issues.

KIDSPHERE NETWORK

The Kidsphere Network is a growing international

network of students and teachers. The main Kidsphere list is mainly for teachers. It links classrooms looking to cooperate on projects. Another list, called simply Kids, is for kid-to-kid communications.

To subscribe to Kidsphere send e-mail to: kid sphere-request@vms.cis.pitt.edu. In the body of your message write: subscribe kidsphere [your name]. Subscribe to Kids by sending e-mail to: kids@vms. cis.pitt.edu. In the body of your message write: subscribe kids [your name].

MORE SOURCES FOR ONLINE PROJECTS

The Global Network Academy
  (http://uu-gna.mit.edu:8001/uu-gna/)
Internet Projects Registry
  (http://gsn.org/gsn/gsn.projects.registry.html)
Educational Resources
  (http://www.acm.cps.msu.edu/~spiveyed/
  Education.html)
Busy Teachers Web Site
  (http://www.gatech.edu/lcc/idt/Students/Cole/
  Proj/K-12/TOC.html)

ONLINE HELP WITH OFFLINE PROJECTS

The online world can also help you with offline school projects. There are lots of cool sites where you can check out science projects and other assignments kids have posted. Check out some of these sources!

MINNESOTA CYBERFAIR
(http://www.isd77.k12.mn.us/resources/cf/
welcome.html)
This Web site is an excellent guide on how to do an

experimental science project. It reviews all the steps you need to do to conduct a successful experiment—hypothesis, procedure, data, observations, and conclusions. It's also a great place to look for science project ideas. Lots of kids have posted their projects here.

SCIENCE FAIR HOME PAGE
(http://www.stemnet.nf.ca/~jbarron/scifair.html)
This home page may be the best-kept secret in cyberspace. When we visited it, it had registered just over a thousand uses in the previous two months—far too little traffic for this really cool and useful site. There are hundreds of ideas for science projects for every area of science and every grade level—and lots of links to other science project and science fair resources on the Web!

CYBERSPACE MIDDLE SCHOOL SCIENCE FAIR
(http://www.scri.fsu.edu/~dennisl/special/
sciencefair95.html)
Thnking about a science fair project? Need ideas? At the Cyberspace Middle School Science Fair you'll find practical hints for selecting and completing science fair projects. Read descriptions of possible projects, try them out, or try to improve on them. You can even submit your project for judging.

AMATEUR SCIENCE PROJECTS
(http://www.eskimo.com/~billb/amasci.html)
Bill Beaty, who runs this home page, describes himself as "a closet physics teacher" and says "the WWW finally gives me an outlet for all the neat teaching ideas I come up with but which would otherwise go unused." It also gives him an outlet for a

lot of incredibly complex experiments with big expensive equipment, almost all of which are about blowing up stuff. The disclaimer for one project starts off, "The watergun is a full-fledged cannon and must be treated as such. And these are not the only hazards." Hmmm. Well, at least now we know why Bill is only allowed to teach physics in a closet. But never mind all that. There are also directions for safer—and simpler!—projects like lava lamps, electrostatic generators, etc.

OTHER GREAT SITES

California State Science Fair
   (http://www.usc.edu/CMSI/CalifSF/)

Fun Science Fair Projects
   (http://outcast.gene.com/ae/RC/BAP/CT/
   fun_science_fair_projects.html)

London Science & Technology Fair
   (http://quark.physics.uwo.ca/sfair/scifr.html)

Nick Gidzak Page
   (http://megamach.portage.net:80/~bgidzak/
   nick.html)

Practical Hints for Science Fair Projects
   (http://www.scri.fsu.edu/~dennis/special/
   sf_hints.html)

Science Fair Home Page
   (http://www.scienceworld.bc.ca/Science_Fair/
   Index.html)

Science Fair Project Steps
   (http://www.isd77.k12.mn.us/resources/cf/
   steps.html)

Science Web Page
   (http://calvin.stemnet.nf.ca/~gcoombes/
   science.html)

Virtual Science and Mathematics Fair
  (http://www.educ.wsu.edu/fair_95/index.html)

What Makes a Good Project?
  (http://www.isd77.k12.mn.us/resources/cf/
  goodproject.html)

TOP SCHOOL SITES

Does your school have a Web site? More and more
schools are setting up home pages on the Web every
day. And many of the best school sites feature online
projects you can do by yourself or in collaboration
with others. Check out some of these cool school
sites.

ARBOR HEIGHTS SCHOOL
(http://www.halcyon.com/arborhts/
arborhts.html)
Seattle's Arbor Heights School was one of the first
elementary schools on the World Wide Web, and it's
still one of the best student sites online. You can read
the latest issue of the staff and student produced
Junior Seahawk newsletter, or the Cool Writers' magazine, a page linking great student writing all over
the Web. You'll also find links to news and weather
information for Seattle. One group of third graders
have compiled the Room 12 Top Ten List, which is
an ever-changing list of links to the kids' favorite
Web hangouts. When we visited, they had links to
WebCrawler searching, the film *The Indian in the Cup-
board*, R. L. Stine's "Goosebumps" books, and—sur-
prise—the Mariners Internet Image Archive for
pictures of Seattle's hometown baseball team!

BLACKBURN HIGH SCHOOL
(http://www.ozemail.com.au/~bhs56/)
Worried that American schools aren't as good as schools in other countries? Then stay away from this school home page from suburban Melbourne, Australia—it will only convince you that it's true. This professional-quality site is incredibly rich and deep with lots of links to a dizzying array of cool and useful stuff. The school is renowned for its students high academic performance and for excellence in music—you can download sound clips of Blackburn's orchestra, stage band, singers, and more. You'll also find lots of student essays on literature, a good collection of reference resources, and lots of pictures of the Blackburn kids hard at work or play. We were going to download a bunch of them, but we figured all the kids would probably have great hair, straight teeth, and no zits. We got depressed just thinking about it and decided to move on.

CYBERSPACE MIDDLE SCHOOL
(http://www.scri.fsu.edu/~dennisl/CMS.html)
Over one thousand kids every week visit the Cyberspace Middle School. It features links to schools and classes that have home pages or online projects, educational activities for middle school students, and lots of links to Web locations with information useful to students.

EASTCHESTER MIDDLE SCHOOL
(http://www.westnet.com/~rickd/index.html)
A lot of school Web sites feature links to other sites that students can use for schoolwork. Eastchester Middle School, which is just north of New York City, is no exception. They've got a great list of links. But

what makes this site really special is the original material put up by Eastchester's students. Sixth grader Joanna Michalowski's "A Journey to India" has her journal and beautiful photographs from her trip. Eighth grader Joseph Mariani was one of only thirty-four U.S. students selected to serve as a people-to-people student ambassador to Western Europe—his photographic scrapbook of France, Germany, Spain, and Switzerland is also online here. There's also plenty of artwork, stories, and opinion pieces by the kids at Eastchester.

THE FALCON'S NEST
(http://www2.northstar.k12.ak.us/schools/upk/upk.home.html)
The Flacon's Nest is the Web home of University Park Elementary School in Fairbanks, Alaska. You'll find lots of interesting information about Alaska, including links to sites about the northern lights and dogsled racing. There's also plenty of information about the school and students, including projects on ice art, traditional native wood mask carving and transformation myths and masks, and links to some of the students' personal home pages and instructions for finding an Alaskan key pal. Check out Greetings in Many Languages, where you'll find pictures and audio of University Park's multilingual students welcoming you in lots of different tongues, including Russian, Spanish, Yupik, and Polish.

THOMAS JEFFERSON HIGH SCHOOL FOR SCIENCE AND TECHNOLOGY
(http://www.tjhsst.edu/)
Thomas Jefferson High had more National Merit semifinalists than any other school in the United

States last year—for the sixth year in a row! These kids are no dummies, and their Web page proves it. Jefferson High has a large number of technology labs (astronomy, computer assisted design, industrial automation and robotics, video technology, and more), each with its own Web page. There are also pages for the *tjToday* student newspaper, a JPEG art gallery with student and faculty artwork, and links to student home pages, many of which include students' resumes. Resumes? OK, so maybe these kids are a little too smart for their own good. Regardless of the few show-offs, it's still a terrific Web site. Resumes?

WEB66
(http://web66.coled.umn.edu/)
The Univeristy of Minnesota's College of Education and Human Development Web66 project has lots of resources for schools. It also maintains the International WWW Schools Registry, the biggest list anywhere of wired schools. Click on a map of the United States (or the world) and you'll find hypertext links to schools with their own Web sites. The Web66 Classroom Internet Server Cookbook gives recipes with step-by-step instructions for setting up a Web server on a Macintosh or Windows 95 computer, with hypertext links to every ingredient you will need.

MORE COOL SCHOOL SITES

Buckman Elementary School (Portland, Oregon)
  (http://buckman.pps.k12.or.us/buckman.html)

Delmar Elementary School (Delmar, Maryland)
  (http://shore1.intercom.net/local/weeg/)

DuPont Hadley Middle School (Nashville, Tennessee)
(http://www.tbr.state.tn.us/~heltonj/duponthp.html)

Hillside Elementary School (Cottage Grove, Minnesota)
(http://hillside.coled.umn.edu/)

Jordan Middle School (Palo Alto, California)
(http://www.jordan.palo-alto.ca.us/)

L'Ouverture Computer Technology Magnet (Wichita, Kansas)
(http://www.louverture.com/index.html)

North Hagerstown High School (Hagerstown, Maryland)
(http://www.fred.net/nhhs/nhhs.html)

Oak Mountain Intermediate School (Birmingham, Alabama)
(http://www.tech-comm.com/omis/)

Ralph Bunche School (New York City)
(http://mac94.ralphbunche.rbs.edu/)

Stewart Middle School (Tacoma, Washington)
(http://www.stewart.edu/)

Sullivan Middle School (Rock Hill, South Carolina)
(http://Web.InfoAve.Net/~cs4603suafos/index.html)

Wilcox Elementary School (Wilcox, Saskatchewan, Canada)
(http://wilcox.unibase.com/welcome.html)

MERRY CHRISTMAS TO YOUR KEY PALS— WHEREVER THEY ARE! - - - - - - - - - - - -

E-mail allows you to send and receive letters from kids in

countries all around the world. English has emerged as the most commonly used language in cyberspace. Still, being online gives you an opportunity to learn a few phrases in lots of local tongues. Becky Ross, a third grade teacher in Benicia, California, has accumulated the following list which will enable you to say "Seasons Greetings" to your key pal, wherever he or she might be!

Afrikaans—*Een Plesierige Kerfees*

Armenian—*Shenoraavor Nor Dari yev Pari Gaghand*

Azeri—*Tezze Iliniz Yahsi Olsun*

Basque—*Zorionstsu Eguberri. Zoriontsu Urte Berri On*

Bohemian—*Vesele Vanoce*

Breton—*Nedeleg laouen na bloavezh mat*

Bulgarian—*Tchestita Koleda; Tchestito Rojdestvo Hristovo*

Chinese:
  Mandarin—*Kung His Hsin Nien bing Chu Shen Tan*
  Cantonese—*Gun Tso Sun Tan'Gung Haw Sun*

Cornish—*Nadelik looan na looan blethen noweth*

Cree—*Mitho Makosi Kesikansi*

Croatian—*Sretan Bozic*

Czech—*Prejeme Vam Veséle Vanoce*

Danish—*Gldelig Jul*

Dutch—*Vrolijk Kerstfeest en een Gelukkig Nieuwjaar!*

English—*merry Christmas*

Esperanto—*Gajan Kristnaskon*

Estonian—*Roomsaid Joulu Puhi*

Finnish—*Hauskaa joulua*

French—*Joyeux Noël*

Frisian—*Noflike Krystdagen en in protte Lok en Seine yn it Nije Jier!*

German—*fröliche Weihnachten*

Greek—*Kala Christouyenna!*

Hawaiian—*Mele Kilikimaka me ka Hauoli Makahiki ho*

Hebrew—*Mo'adim Lesimkha. Chena tova*

Hindi—*Shub Naya Baras*

Hungarian—*Kellemes Karacsonyi unnepeket*

Icelandic—*Gledileg Jol*

Indonesian—*Selamat Hari Natal*

Irish—*Nodlaig mhaith chugnat*

Italian—*buone feste Natale*

Japanese—*Shinnen omedeto. Kurisumasu Omedeto*

Korean—*Sung Tan Chuk Ha*

Latvian—*Priecigus Ziemas Svetkus un Laimigu Jauno Gadu*

Lithuanian—*Linksmu Kaledu*

Manx—*Nollick ghennal as blein vie noa*

Maori—*Meri Kirihimete*

Marathi—*Shub Naya Varsh*

Norwegian—*God Jul Og Godt Nytt Aar*

Polish—*Wesolych Swiat Bozego Narodzenia*

Portuguese—*Boas Festas*

Rapa-Nui (Easter Island)—*Mata-Ki-Te-Rangi. Te-Pito-O-Te-Henua*

Romanian—*Sarbatori vesele*

Russian—*Pozdrevlyayu s prazdnikom Rozhdestva is Novim Godom*

Samoan—*La Maunia Le Killisimasi Ma Le Tausaga Fou*

Scottish Gaelic—*Nollaig Chridheil agus Biladhna Mhath Ur*

Serbian—*Hristos se rodi*

Serbo-Croatian—*Sretam Bozic. Vesela Nova Godina*

Sinhalese—*Subha nath thalak Vewa. Subha Aluth Awrudhak Vewa*

Slovak—*Vesele Vianoce. A stastlivy Novy Rok*

Slovene—*Vesele Bozicne. Screcno Novo Leto*

Spanish—*Feliz Navidad*

Swedish—*God jul and (Och) Ett Gott Nytt Ar*

Tagalog—*Maligayamg Pasko. Masaganang Bagong Taon*

Tamil—*Nathar Puthu Varuda Valthukkal*

Turkish—*Noeliniz Ve Yeni Yiliniz Kutlu Olsun*

Ukrainian—*Srozhdestvom Kristovym*

Urdu—*Naya Saal Mubarak Ho*

Vietnamese—*No^ En—French based (Noël)*

  Chu'c Mu`ng Giang Si.nh—*Sino-Vietnamese*

Welsh—*Nadolig Llawen*

THE GREAT INFO SHOWDOWN

History is full of famous showdowns: David versus Goliath. The gunfight at the O.K. Corral. Gary Kasparov versus Deep Blue, the chess-playing computer. The next great showdown may pit the library against the computer.

For years, the library has been the warehouse of

knowledge. Libraries are big, foreboding buildings, piled to the rafters with row upon row of books—each one a tiny piece of the sum of everything human beings have ever thought and done. And tucked way in a tiny corner of the library is the little machine with the power to bring all of those book stacks tumbling down. As the Information Age rushes ahead, the library building may become obsolete. A computer hooked to the Internet promises to put a library on every desk.

THE LIBRARY VERSUS THE NET

Legend has it that years ago, there was a great black railroad construction worker named John Henry, who claimed he could drive a steel spike into solid rock just as fast as a newly-invented steam drill. According to the famous folk song:

> *John Henry told his captain,*
> *"A man ain't nothin' but a man,*
> *And before I'd let your steam drill beat me down*
> *I'd die with this hammer in my hand.*
> *I'd die with my hammer in my hand."*

True to his word, John Henry won the race against the steam drill using just a sledgehammer. But he had to work so hard to do so that—also true to his word—he died with his hammer in his hand.

Is the Internet the steam drill? Are librarians John Henry? Where can you find facts faster, online or in the library? There was only one way to find out. So one chilly day last February, we challenged two groups of kids at Beers Street Middle School in Hazlet, New Jersey, to find out in the Great Info Showdown.

Four seventh-grade classes and one eighth-grade class worked on the project. They were divided into two groups. The first group prowled the stacks looking for answers in books, magazines, newspapers—any printed material was fair game. The second group logged on to the Net and—fingers flying—pointed and clicked their way to paydirt. Students with stopwatches timed how long it took to find the answers to more than a dozen questions in science, geography, history, literature, and more.

The first question was "What's the tallest volcano in the world and where is it located?" The students working on the Internet used a search engine to surf their way to Volcano World (http://volcano.und.nodak.edu), a Web site run by the University of North Dakota. After four and a half minutes, they learned that Ojos del Salado in northern Chile is the tallest volcano in the world. The library team had a much easier time of it, learning the answer in the *Guinness Book of Answers* in just under two minutes. Score one for John Henry. Library 1, Internet 0.

Next, the kids were asked to name the planet with the most moons. The ink-and-paper team found the answer—Saturn—in two and a half minutes. The Internet team found the answer just as quickly at the National Space Science Data Center Planetary Sciences Web site (http://nssdc.gsfc.nasa.gov/planetary). We called it a tie. Library 2, Internet 1.

Moving from science to literature, the next question was: "Shakespeare wrote three kinds of plays: tragedies, comedies, and histories. Give one example of each." In another virtual dead heat, the library gang took three minutes to find the answer in the card catalogue. The cyberkids moused on over to The Collected Works of William Shakespeare on the

Web (http://www.gh.cs.usyd.edu.au/~matty/Shake speare/) within seven seconds of the library team— close enough to call it a tie. Library 3, Internet 2.

Who is the president of Mexico? Our digital infonauts used Yahoo! (http://www.yahoo.com/Regional/Countries/Mexico/Government/) to find out that Ernesto Zedillo is *el Presidente* of our neighbor south of the border. They took three minutes to unearth this tidbit, while noting that they could have found the answer more quickly except their 14.4 modem was slow in connecting them. No points were subtracted for whining, but the library kids trounced their online competitors anyway, finding the answer in the *1996 World Almanac* in one minute forty-six seconds. Library 4, Internet 2.

Things started looking bleak for the cybersearchers when the question was, "When was the Battle of Gettysburg fought? Who were the winning and losing generals?" The kids in the library found the answer in the encyclopedia in one and a half minutes. The Internet kids took four minutes to find out the Battle of Gettysburg was fought on July 1 to 3, 1863, with Robert E. Lee's Confederates losing to Union general George G. Meade's Army of the Potomac. Library 5, Internet 2.

And like Gettysburg, the battle between the page turners and the mouse clickers raged on. The library searchers found the answers first to "What is blood pressure and how is it measured?" "When and where was the first Super Bowl?" and "What Supreme Court decision struck down school segregation?"

The cybersearchers came out ahead on "There are three classifications of clouds—name them" and

"Which amendment to the Constitution gave eighteen-year-olds the right to vote?"

There were dead heats on "What is the Pythagorean theorem?" and "Dinosaurs roamed the earth during the Triassic and Jurassic geologic periods. When did primitive man arrive?"

When the dust cleared, the library searchers hung on to win, beating the upstart cybersurfers, 10–6. But like John Henry, the library may be enjoying its last hours in the sun. Teacher Eileen M. Bendixsen, who coached the Internet team, pointed out that for many of the students, it was their first time on the Net. The moral of the story? The library team may have won this round, but like John Henry, they may die trying to keep up. As more and more kids become as comfortable online as they are prowling the stacks, look for the time spent looking up information online to drop dramatically.

Perhaps even more telling was the reaction of the students to the Great Info Showdown. "The students in several of my classes would like to know when we can go back online," said Ms. Bendixsen. "A few students said they wished they had been on the Internet team."

A few comments from the contestants at Beers Street Middle School:

- "I would rather go online because you don't have to leave the house and it's quicker and much better."

- "I think the Info Showdown was great. I've started using the Internet for projects and pretty much loved every moment."

- "I thought the Internet was interesting and a different way to do work/research."

- "I liked the project because I got to see what you could get to with the Internet. You could get any information."
- "I liked the Internet better. It was easier to use and for me it was quicker."

Ms. Bendixsen also asked her classes if they were connected to the Internet at home and had a report due on Friday would they choose to go online for their information, use the library, or a combination of both? Thirteen students said they would choose the library. Fifty-five students chose the Internet to do their report. "Several stated that they liked the convenience of having the Internet in their home and not having to go to the library," reported Ms. Bendixsen. "Many felt that they could get more information faster online." Said one student: "I would choose to go online because I hate using libraries. It's a waste of time because the book I need is always out."

That throbbing sound you hear is John Henry's heart pounding at full throttle as his fingers fly through the card catalogue.

Stress-Proof Research Papers

"I use the Internet for school projects and especially for researching topics for debating. We are the only public school in the New England Debating Society, and we have sent debaters literally all over the world."

—NORMA JEAN MAC PHEE,
Sydney, Nova Scotia

Q: What are the four most dreaded words in the English language?

A: Research paper.

I know, I know. That's only two words. Have two more.

A: Oral report.

Feel the hair standing up on the back of your neck?

Breaking out in a cold sweat? Don't. Here are four more words to calm you down: "Don't panic. Log on!"

BEATING RESEARCH PHOBIA

Just the word *research* is enough to strike fear into the hearts of most students. It doesn't have to be that way. When you get an assignment to do a major paper or oral report, the first and most important piece of advice is not to be intimidated. *Research* is just another word for *curiosity*. If you're curious about something and take the time to learn more—no matter how you do it—you're a researcher. And thanks to the huge number of resources available online, you might actually find you enjoy doing research. OK, maybe not. But it sure beats breaking rocks in the hot sun all day.

Think of it this way: Research doesn't have to mean going to the library—or even going online. You do research every day. Turning on the radio to hear a weather report is research. So is picking up *TV Guide* to see what time a program comes on. You're doing research at this very moment. You want to know how to find information online, and you're curious enough to "research" it by reading this book.

When you think of it as an ordinary everyday activity, the idea of doing research sounds a lot less terrifying, doesn't it? Doing a research paper or oral report isn't very much different from the activities we described above. If you break it down, doing a research project boils down to five easy steps:

1. Ask a question.
2. Identify your research tools.

3. Plan your research.

4. Collect information.

5. Prepare your report.

You go through the research process dozens of times every day without even thinking about it. Say, for example, you want to know, "What time and where is *Ace Ventura* playing? (Step 1. Ask a question.) You could find out by looking in the newspaper or calling your local movie theater. (Step 2. Identify your research tools.) You then realize calling the theater down the street may be a waste of time, since you don't have any idea whether the movie's even playing there. (Step 3. Plan your research.) So you look at the timetable in the paper and find out the movie is playing at the mall at 5:30 P.M. (Step 4. Collect information.) So you call your friends and say, "*Ace Ventura* is playing at the Cinema Odeon Hundredplex at 5:30. Meet me there at 5:15." (Step 5. Prepare your report.)

Now, if only you could get your teacher to accept *that* as a research project.

Let's put the same process to work for school.

1. ASK A QUESTION
Ask a question—any question! What do you want to know? Will humans ever be able to time travel? What would happen if the world stopped spinning? Do rainbows touch the ground? Why are tall mountains always covered with snow? Asking a question that you don't know the answer to is the first step in designing a research project.

2. IDENTIFY YOUR RESEARCH TOOLS

Once you have figured out what you want to know, you can start to think about the best way to find the answer. When you wanted to know "what time does the movie start?" you simply looked it up in the movie timetable in the newspaper. If you're going online to do a research paper or oral report for school, however, you might need several different sources of information—encyclopedias, newspaper articles, books, e-mail interviews, etc.

3. PLAN YOUR RESEARCH

Once you're online, you have an embarrassment of riches for any research project. The trick will be figuring out how much information you will need and where you are going to find it. For a major research assignment, multiple sources will be needed—online and off. An important piece of the research plan is to make sure there are enough sources of information about your topic before you take on an assignment. You don't want to be stuck with a question you can't answer. Another important piece of the planning process is to leave yourself enough time to research your subject and have enough time left over to write your report.

4. COLLECT INFORMATION

For many researchers, this is the fun part of the job. Doing the actual digging—hunting around online, uncovering facts and information you never knew before—is like being a detective or an explorer. If you choose a topic you're interested in, research will never seem like a chore. Depending on the subject, you can use "primary" or "secondary" sources of information. Primary sources are facts you gather yourself through experiments, observations, or personal experience. Interviews, historical documents, photographs, official records, and documents are also considered primary resources. Secondary sources are someone else's experiments, observations, or experiences. Books, articles, and encyclopedias are all secondary sources, since they describe someone or something else. Another way to think of it is firsthand and secondhand information. When you begin a research project, try to figure out what primary and secondary sources you will be able to use.

5. PREPARE YOUR REPORT

I'm not going to try to convince you that writing a report is a lot of fun. Some people enjoy writing. Some people would rather—well—break rocks in the hot sun all day. But whether you love it or hate it, you can still be good at it if you follow a plan. Remember that the key to good writing is rewriting—don't try to write an entire report all at once. Start with an outline or a sketch, fill in as many of the details as possible, then do a first draft. Allow yourself time to rewrite the draft so it's smooth and makes sense. If you're writing an oral report, think about visual aids—charts, graphs, and other devices—that will help illustrate the points you are trying to make.

FINDING THE KILLER IDEA

Sometimes your teacher may not give you a specific assignment. (Don't you just hate that?) Instead, you might be asked to come up with an idea for a science project. Or you might be told to report on a subject you're interested in. If you're stuck for an idea, don't panic. A little brainstorming will help you find the perfect subject.

If your assignment is to come up with a general research project, then anything goes. Think about subjects in school that interest you. Do you like math? Music? Science? History? If you can choose any subject for a research project, do yourself a favor and pick one you're interested in. If you're going to have to do the work anyway, it might as well be something fun that you're looking forward to learning more about, right?

So what do you want to know more about? Are you interested in horses? NBA basketball? Dinosaurs? Space exploration? Snakes and reptiles No subject is too silly or too weird when you're just brainstorming. Just think of general subjects that you're curious about and write them down as they pop into your head.

BRAINSTORMING ONLINE
The World Wide Web is a *great* brainstorming machine. If you're trying to come up with an idea for a science project, check out one of the science Web pages mentioned earlier in this book. A few minutes of Web surfing might be all you need to get you thinking about great research projects! Or try one of the search engines like Yahoo or Alta Vista. You just might find a home page that gives you some ideas. Jot down a few ideas that interest you (and bookmark the home pages that helped you). You can check out online message boards. Look at some projects other kids have done, or post a message asking for suggestions for ideas that have worked for other kids.

ZEROING IN

OK, so let's say you've decided you want to do your research project on "outer space." That's a pretty big subject. Some astronomers spend their entire lives taking up space. And while you may be curious, you're not sure you want to sign up for the rest of your life—you just need a research paper by next Friday. What to do?

Narrow your focus. Outer space is infinitely large, and there's a mind-boggling amount of information about the subject out there. The next step is to figure out what interests you about space. Start by asking yourself what you really want to know. Do you want to know about stars or planets? Are you curious about the space shuttle? Maybe it's telescopes you're really interested in. Maybe it's UFOs and the possibility of life elsewhere in the universe.

Once you've narrowed your subject, write down some questions you want to know the answers to. If you've decided you want to do a project about space, what do you want to know?

How old is the universe?

How do we know what comets are made of?

What's a black hole?

How do astronauts survive in space?

How long would it take to get to Mars?

Is there intelligent life elsewhere in the universe?

If you find yourself having trouble coming up with questions that you're curious about, take a hint: This is probably not a good subject for you to do for a research project. If you have the chance to choose your topic, picking something you're not interested in is like giving yourself a jail sentence. If no questions come to mind, back up and look for another subject! Hopefully, one of your brainstorm questions will jump out at you as something you're really curious about. When that happens, you've found your research topic!

Before you begin actually doing your research, make sure your question isn't too narrow or too broad. Try to pick a question that you're pretty sure you can find information about. Suppose the question that jumps out at you is: Is there intelligent life elsewhere in the universe? We'd all like to know the answer to that, but you're not going to find the answer even on the Internet! But just because you can't give a definite yes or no answer to a question doesn't mean it's not a good research subject.

Say we decide we want to do *something* about life elsewhere in the universe. Then it's time to narrow our focus to a specific topic that we can actually find information about through research. This is the moment of truth for our project—the Big Question that we want to know the answer to. How about this: What are the odds there is intelligent life elsewhere in the universe?

Liftoff! We have our research subject!

DISASTER CHECK

Before you settle on a research subject, it's important to be reasonably sure that you'll be able to find enough information to address your question. As long as you can find three or four sources to cite for your project, you're probably OK. This may seem like a boring and annoying step, but it's *nothing* compared to the panic that will hit you when it's the night before your deadline and you can't find anything about your subject to write about. Trust us. Been there, done that. Got the scars to prove it.

Here's where a quick trip to the online encyclopedia can be really helpful. On AOL, there are two encyclopedias available, the *Compton's Living Encyclopedia* and the *Concise Columbia Encyclopedia*. Let's check there (key word: Encyclopedia) to make sure we're not headed down a blind alley.

Compton's gives you the ability to search every single article for key words or phrases you're interested in. Let's click on Search All Text and type in a few words about our subject. Our project is to look into the odds that there is life elsewhere in the universe, so we type in "extraterrestrial life" and click on the button that says List All Articles.

Bingo!

Compton's search engine found twelve articles on extraterrestrial life. Here's what the first one says:

Extraterrestrial life. The search for life away from planet Earth has been called a science without a subject matter. Despite the countless hours that dedicated scientists and amateurs alike have spent searching the skies, there is no evidence that life exists anywhere in the universe except on Earth. Exobiology is a branch of biology that deals with the search for extraterrestrial life, especially intelligent life, outside our solar system. Exobiology is sometimes called xenobiology or astrobiology.

So we've already learned that there's a name for our subject. It's called exobiology. Another one of the articles listed is titled "Search for Extraterrestrial Intelligence." Let's check that one out.

> *Search for Extraterrestrial Intelligence (SETI), an organized search for signs of intelligent life in other parts of the universe besides Earth. It began actively in 1960 when American astronomer Frank Drake searched for radio signals from two nearby stars. Once ridiculed, the search has grown in support, including the NASA-sponsored project, SETI. It is based on the assumption that any technologically advanced civilization would produce electromagnetic signals to communicate with other intelligent civilizations.*

Now we're really getting somewhere! Not only does our subject have a name, but there are definitely experiments going on to find out the answer to our question. We can be pretty confident now that we're not going to have any major trouble finding information about our topic. A quick search in the *Columbia Encyclopedia* on AOL shows more articles about exobiology, including one about the scientist Carl Sagan, who has spent much of his career trying to answer our research question.

PLAN YOUR SEARCH

Everything is coming together now. We've got our subject, we've got a thesis question to explore, and we've got a pretty good idea that we're not looking for a needle in a haystack. Time to get to work. All that's left to do is figure out where to start. Hmmm. OK. Where *do* you start? The online encyclopedia gave us some leads about exobiology, SETI, and Carl Sagan. That's a good start. But we're going to need a lot more information.

We need to plan our research. Start by making a list of where to look for information. The online encyclopedia was our first stop. Where else can we look?

Remember what we learned about the World Wide Web and search engines? Armed with a few helpful search terms, we can look for Web sites about our subject. By pointing our browser to Yahoo (http://www.yahoo.com), we can see what's out there. Maybe we won't find intelligent life elsewhere in the universe, but maybe we'll find some on the Web!

A search of the phrase "extraterrestrial life" turns up three Web sites on our subject. One is for the SETI Institute, and the other two are for something called The Planetary Society. These sound pretty promising!

Another place to look for information is Usenet newsgroups and online forums. A search of Usenet newsgroups turns up something called alt.aliens.visitors. But a quick check of the frequently asked questions (FAQs) shows this newsgroup describes itself as being about "Space aliens on earth! Abduction! Gov't coverup!" Hmmm. Maybe it's better to look for information someplace where people sound a little less, er, excitable. Don't you think?

Back on AOL, there are hundreds of special interest groups and forums. Maybe one of them has some useful information. We can use the Directory of Services to find areas that might be useful for our topic. By searching for areas about space it turns out there are twenty-six areas that have something about space, including the Astronomy Club and the National Space Society.

A quick visit to the National Space Society (key word: Space) shows they have message boards with lively discussions on dozens of topics related to space exploration. It turns out there's even a message folder about the search for extraterrestrial life! By posting in the message boards, maybe someone who knows about the subject will come forward with a source of information we haven't discovered yet.

Subj: Exobiology
Date: 96-01-21 20:01:09 EST
From: RPondiscio
Posted on: America Online

For a school research project on the possibility of life elsewhere in the universe, I'm looking for online or Internet resources on the subject. Can someone suggest Web sites or other sources where I might find credible information on the odds of extraterrestrial life?

A visit to AOL's newsstand turns up lots of newspapers and magazines to search through for recent articles. Since our paper is on a science subject, it makes the most sense to look for magazines that cover science. As luck would have it, AOL has *Scientific American* online. A quick key-word search of back issues for "extraterrestrial life" turns up a long article from October 1994 by Carl Sagan. And not only is this article about our topic, but it has a bibliography at the end that lists over two dozen articles about the subject!

So we've found the following sources of information to explore:

- *Compton's Encyclopedia* on AOL
- the SETI Institute, and The Planetary Society on the Web
- the National Space Society message boards
- *Scientific American*, October 1994

And if we need more, three out of four of our sources lead to other resources we can use!

SEARCH YOUR PLAN

OK, so we have covered most of our bases. We know there's lots of material on our subject. And we know where to look. Now we just need to plan so we have plenty of time to explore all the sources of information we've found—to surf the Web sites we've identified, download the article we found on AOL (remember to download first, and read offline to save money!), and plenty of time to write about what we find out. Also remember to check back from time to time on the message boards you left questions on, and check your e-mail to see if someone has written to you with suggestions.

There are no rules for making a research plan. You have to know your own work habits. Do you enjoy writing? Does it come easily to you? Then you can spend more time researching and less time writing. If writing doesn't come easily to you, you might want to budget extra time for that. You know the date your assignment is due, so work backward from there and figure out how much time you'll need to get everything done.

WHO DO YOU TRUST?

The Internet is a terrific source. You don't have to be a computer geek to share what you know with the world. Unfortunately, you don't have to have a clue, either. Let's face it, there's more than a few crackpots out there, and a surprising number of them seem to be in cyberspace.

This presents a problem for the would-be infonaut.

Who do you trust? A topic like the search for extra-terrestrial life is one of those subjects that brings the goofballs out in droves. It's important when doing research to think about the credibility of the information you find. This is true no matter where you're doing research, but it's especially true online. On the subject of extraterrestrial life, for example, you're more likely to find serious, authoritative information at the NASA Web site than on a message board set up by fans of *Star Trek* or *The X-Files*.

When you come across information that seems useful to your project, it's a good idea to ask yourself, "Is this reliable? What are the authors' credentials? Do they have any reason to mislead me? Why should I take their word for it? What proof do they have? How do *I* know *they* know what they're talking about?"

It's also a good idea to make sure the information you have uncovered is current. You always want your research to be as up-to-date as possible. That's one of the best parts of searching for information online—in the time it takes to print and publish a book, the information inside it can get very old and musty.

EXPERT TIPS FOR SUPERSEARCHERS

Before you begin hunting for information online, get a few things ready to keep you organized.

- Keep a notebook by your computer to write down things you want to remember, like the names of online places where you found useful articles. Bookmark the URLs of useful Web sites or jot them down. You might also want to write down the names and URLs of other sites that you want to visit later on but don't have time to see right now.

- Keep a few blank disks ready to make backups of articles and information you find and save. Teachers are getting more and more savvy about computers. They're not going to buy it if you say "my hard drive crashed" any more than they're likely to accept "the dog ate my homework." Back up your work often!

- Create files to organize and store the information you find online. You can organize these files however you wish. You might keep a file called Articles and Information for newspaper and magazine articles or information from online encyclopedias and reference books that you want to refer to later. A second folder called Artwork could be a place to store any pictures and graphics you want to use in your report. Another folder called Primary Sources is where you might store any e-mail that you send and receive from experts and logs of online interviews you do. Keep a separate disk called Final Report to store your own writing. It's *very* important to keep your own original thoughts and words separate from articles that you download. This way there's no chance that you'll get your words confused with someone else's. This will make your project plagiarism proof.

- When you're searching for information online, saving articles and information onto folders on your hard drive or on disks can save you money if you're paying by the hour to be online. Download the articles that look the most helpful and read them offline. Use your online time for searching, not reading. This will keep your online charges to a minimum.

Setting up an organized file system before you begin your research will help you stay focused and keep track of the information you find. This way, when it comes time to write your paper, you'll have everything you need and know exactly where to find it.

WRITING YOUR REPORT

Once you've got all your material, it's time to write your report. This is a major stress-producer for a lot of kids. If you've approached the rest of the project in an organized way, you'll find you're a lot more relaxed and confident when the time comes to write your paper or prepare your presentation. Whatever you do, try to leave yourself plenty of time for writing. Organize all your facts and conclusions in an outline or on notecards before beginning. Keep your main points in mind and dump anything that doesn't get right to the heart of the question you asked when you began the project.

Don't try to sit down and write your report all at once. Leave plenty of time for a first draft, a second draft—as many drafts as you need to write a smooth, smart paper. Don't be afraid to ask others for suggestions once you've got a finished draft. Sometimes, when you learn a lot about a subject, you start to assume that everyone else knows as much about your subject as you do. That can mean big gaps in your paper. Someone who hasn't done the research you've done can usually read your report and tell you whether they understand the points you're trying to make.

If you need tips on writing, consult some of these online writer's resources:

The Write Place
(http://www.rio.com/~wplace/)

Writer's Block Home Page
(http://www.accsyst.com/writers/bbs.htm)

Writer's Resources on the Web
(http://www.interlog.com/~ohi/www/
writesource.html)

Writing Tips, Guides, and Advice
(http://www.missouri.edu/~wleric/
writehelp.html

The Coolest Online
Hangouts

"I think that this Internet thing is so cool! I live in what seems to be the smallest town on earth, and nothing ever happens here, so seeing other people and places all over the world is awesome!"

—MEREDITH RAPPAPORT

You know what all work and no play makes. Fortunately, there's more to do online than just look up facts and figures for school. There are hundreds of cool places about sports, hobbies, games, activities, Net surfing, and much more.

Now that our work is over, it's time to kick back and have some fun. This chapter is your guide to the dozens of online sites created just for kids. We'll also look at the fun side of the World Wide Web—it's not all just research and serious stuff!

Web sites range from slick, eye-popping areas produced and run by some of the biggest entertainment companies in the world to a virtual tour of a thirteen-year-old's bedroom in Singapore. We'll take a look at both—and everything in between. We'll also check out lots of sites created and maintained by teenagers.

By sampling a wide variety of what's on the Web, you'll get a feel for what's out there. You might even be inspired to put up a Web site of your own!

ONLINE WEB SITES

AUSTRALIAN KIDS' SITE
(http://www.ozemail.com.au/~ctech/wps.htm)
Check out Australian animals and meet kids from down under at this site set up by kids at Australia's Wangaratta Primary School.

BIG BUS
(http://www.gulf.net/~ptlg/BIGBUS.html)
Big Bus is a free "webzine" (a Web-based magazine) written for well-traveled students who "have a large view of the world they live in." It offers an open forum for students—all articles are written by subscribers. One recent article written by a girl in Thailand described local cuisine: "I hate durian! It must be the smelliest fruit in the world!! Seriously!! It stinks *really* bad. It's not that it's stinky when it's rotten, it's stinky even when it's fresh!!" Who knew?

THE CANADIAN KIDS HOME PAGE
(http://www.onramp.ca/~lowens/107arch.htm)
This elaborate site was built as a jumping-off point for Web surfing for kids from the Great White North, but everyone is welcome and will find it fun and interesting. There are hot links galore pointing to

sites about animals, music, sports, school, other sites by and for kids—each one described to let you know if you'll find info about Canada, pictures, or sounds. If you want a Canadian key pal, this is a great place to find one!

THE CAREER EXPLORERS
(http://www.futurescan.com/)
This free webzine for teens provides information on career planning. The first issue, "I Want to Be a Veterinarian," was full of information for aspiring animal doctors, ideas for career-related volunteer work, and more. Follow a large-animal veterinarian in Frederick, Maryland, as he conducts a herd check, including fun and glamorous tasks like doing rectal palpation on cows, untwisting their fourth stomachs, and deworming heifers. Hmmm. When's the issue on astronauts coming out?

CHESS SERVER GAME PAGE
(http://www.willamette.edu/wdbin/starter.pl)
The Chess Server is an experimental Web server that lets you play chess on the Web against a live opponent. Multiple games (up to an artificial limit of ten right now) can be going simultaneously, and all games can be watched by any number of people.

CYBERKIDS
(http://www.cyberkids.com)
CyberKids is a quarterly online magazine by kids and for kids. It offers fiction, art, and news articles. There's also an online art gallery; a Young Composers area that lets you upload samples of your own music for others to hear; games; the CyberKids Con-

nection, a global kids' community; and the Launch-pad—a list of other good kids sites.

DROOL
**(http://www.mit.edu:8001/afs/athena.mit.edu/
user/j/b/jbreiden/game/entry.html)**
How can you not love a Web site with a name like Drool? It's an interactive story where you take on the character of a dog (that's the drool part), trying to return a thrown stick to your master. You get to decide what kind of dog you want to be. Then you control the dog's movements, turning east or west, choosing to look at objects, and playing with other dogs in the park—all in an attempt to locate the missing stick and bring it back to your master, yapping and drooling all the way.

EDGE
(http://www.jayi.com/jayi/Fishnet/Edge/)
Edge, which calls itself "the high performance electronic magazine for students," lives up to its hype—it's the slickest, smartest webzine for kids anywhere. "Our job," said the editor, "is to give you ideas for ways to think and learn, whether that means introducing you to a summer program you didn't know about or turning you on to a book you've never read. *Edge* readers are cutting-edge teenagers. You have the edge on others, and this electronic magazine is here to help you keep that edge sharp." The debut issue featured interesting and controversial articles about military schools, Ritalin, racism, and other subjects. Linked to FishNet (see below), a new issue of *Edge* goes online every other month.

ETHAN RANDALL'S "MY ROOM" VIRTUAL TOUR
(http://www.singnet.com.sg/~erandall/me.aiff)
Don't let Bart Simpson's scowling face and the DO NOT DISTURB sign on Ethan's door put you off. You're always welcome on this tour of his room. Ethan used to live in New York and Los Angeles; now he lives in Singapore. He's posted an image map of his room—click anywhere on the map and you can see Ethan's posters, his TV, and stereo. Click to turn right, or left, and you might catch a glimpse of Ethan's dog, Brenda, sleeping on the bed. Sign the guest book before you leave!

FIRST FLIGHT
(http://www.firstflight.com/flt1.html)
Want to take flying lessons? This Web site takes you through the preflight instruction pilots have to complete. You'll see a full cockpit instrument panel, checklists for starting engines, communications, take-off checklist, and before- and after-landing checklists. You can take off, fly, turn, climb, and descend.

FISHNET
(http://www.jayi.com/sbi/Open.html)
A World Wide Web gathering place for teenagers, featuring an interactive magazine for teens! Check out StreetSpeak for the latest slang; check out the Weird Fact of the Day (each of the more than two hundred lashes on each eye is shed every three to five months), and much more.

FREEZONE
(http://www.freezone.com)
Despite the name, Freezone isn't free. As Alanis Morissette might say, "Isn't it ironic?" Inside you'll find

Flash, Freezone's monthly webzine. Center features games and a chance to chat with other kids around the world. Mind is Freezone's learning center. The Market is an online kids catalog with computer equipment, clothes, books, music, and toys. World links to the top Web sites and lets you create your own Web site using Home Page Builder. Freezone *is* free if you get there using CompuServe's Internet in a Box for Kids or via CompuServe. Other users pay a flat fee of $4.95 per month. It's a cool site, but with so much great stuff on the Web for free, pass unless you're a CompuServe member.

GLOBAL SHOW-N-TELL
(http://www.manymedia.com/show-n-tell)
This site posts artwork submitted by kids as young as two and as old as seventeen.

HANGMAN
(http://arachnid.cs.cf.ac.uk/htbin/RobH/hangman)
Play hangman against your PC—the challenge gets harder as you get better!

HYPER-GAMES
(http://www.hype.com/game_show/)
Care to buy a vowel, anyone? The games on Hyper-Games are inspired by *Wheel of Fortune, Jeopardy,* and others—and provide hours of fun.

INTERACTIVE WWW GAMES
(http://www.bu.edu/Games/games.html)
Squirreled away deep inside the Web site of the Boston University Scientific Computing and Visualization Group, you'll find a collection of fun and simple

interactive games to play against a computer, including pegs, tic-tac-toe, and a multiplayer hunt the wumpus game, all perfect for procrastinating. Wonder how they get any work done!

INTERESTING DEVICES CONNECTED TO THE NET
(http://www.yahoo.com/Computers_
and_Internet/Internet/Entertainment/
Interesting_Devices_Connected_to_the_Net.)
More mindless fun. This Yahoo list connects you to a wide (and weird) variety of cameras, robotic arms, and other devices wired to the Web, some of which you can control from your keyboard. Then there are links to things like Brian's Phone—and when it last rang, Chris's Web CD Player—see what Chris is listening to, make him listen to something else!, and the ACM Scrolling Sign—a scrolling sign outside some office that will display your message. People have also trained cameras on fish tanks, ant farms, out their windows, etc. You'll also find dozens of soda machines you can dial into to see how many cans of soda are left. Total goofiness.

INTERESTING PLACES FOR KIDS
(http://www.crc.ricoh.com/people/steve/
kids.html)
This plainly labeled Web site has one of the Net's best collections of hot links for kids. Webmaster Stephen Savitzky of Menlo Park, California, warns the list "is primarily for the benefit of my ten-year-old daughter, Katy. Some of the contents may not be suitable for all audiences." Don't worry. Katy has good taste. Categories include Finding Your Way Around the Web, Art and Literature, Music, Arts and Crafts, Toy and Games, Movies and TV Shows—and

there are Web pages set up by (or for) kids and collections of stuff by kids.

INTERNATIONAL COOL KIDS
(http://www.ieighty.net/~ick/)
Matt Garner has put up this Web page with lists of Top Ten Kid Books, Top Ten Kid Internet Sites, Cool Kids Show 'n' Tell, contests and trivia questions, a pen pal list, and lots more. Said modest Matt: "I'm only eleven years old, so this WWW page isn't the greatest." Cut yourself some slack, big guy. It's pretty cool.

INTERNATIONAL KIDS' SPACE
(http://plaza.interport.net:80/kids_space/)
Share your stories and artwork and talk with other kids from around the world. You could spend hours (and probably will!) in this award-winning Web site!

INTERNET FOR KIDS, INC.
(http://www.internet-for-kids.com/)
Get right into the fun of the Internet at this site set up by Dr. Victoria Williams, a teacher and parent. You can practice your Web navigational skills at the Mouse Travel Tips or visit the Gates of No Return and contribute new episodes to a never-ending story.

KID LIST
(http://www.clark.net/pub/journalism/kid.html)
Looking for a place to hang out online? Check out KID, which stands for "Kids Internet Delight." It's a list of hot links to some of the best and best known Web sites for kids.

KIDNEWS
(http://www.vsa.cape.com/~powens/Kidnews.html)

If you're interested in journalism, check out Kid-News—a free news and writing service for students and teachers around the world. You can use stories on the KidNews site for your school newspaper or student newsletters, as long as you credit the author and school, or you can submit your own news stories for others to use.

KIDOPEDIA
(http://rdz.stjohns.edu/kidopedia/)

Kidopedia is an encyclopedia written by kids all over the world. Said the editors: "Imagine the 'lion' entry being written by a kid who sees them roam free in his/her own neighborhood." (Wouldn't that be in the *Kidopedia* entry for "terrified?") "Or how about the entry on 'seals' from a kid who sees them as dinner rather than as something that balances beach balls?" Schools across the world are making their own *Kidopedia*, and the best articles from each are collected at the Best of *Kidopedia*.

KIDPUB
(http://en-garde.com/kidpub)

This popular page allows kids to publish their creative writing and collaborate with kids on stories. To publish your story, just mail it to KidPub@en-garde.com. They'll format it for viewing on the World Wide Web and make a link to it from the KidPub page. Along with your story, you can also publish a brief note introducing yourself.

KIDS' CRAMBO
(http://www.primenet.com/~hodges/
kids_crambo.html)
It's a game, it's a puzzle ... it's just really fun! If
you like playing with words, you'll love games like
crambo, ziggy piggy, and doggerel.

KIDS DID THIS!!
(http://sln.fi.edu/primer/lists/kids.html)
The Franklin Institute offers this hot list of student-
produced Web sites and projects in lots of different
categories: science, art, history, mathematics, language arts, school newspapers, and more.

KIDS' SPACE
(http://plaza.interport.net/kids_space/)
One of the more elaborate online hangouts for kids.
You can register your home page in the Web Kids'
Village, find key pals from all over the world in the
Pen Pal Box and Bulletin Board, post your artwork,
and see other kids' in the Kids' Gallery. One espe-
cially neat feature is the On-Air Concert, featuring
real audio sound files of kids' musical performances.
Lots more!

KIDSCOM
(http://www.kidscom.com)
KidsCom describes itself as a "communications play-
ground," whatever that means. You can read stories
written by other kids, leave some of your own stories
behind, scribble *what* on the Graffiti Wall, learn more
about the Internet, post pictures of your pet in the
Pet Arena, play games, win prizes, and much more.
There's also one of the coolest key pals matchmaking
services on the Net. Language fans take note: you

can access this Web site in four different languages—
English, French, Spanish, and German.

KIDS'CROSSING
(http://rmll.com/~pachecod/kidsnet/ckids.html)
Described as "virtual place for kids under twelve to
hang out," it's designed to be a creative and safe way
for schools and parents to introduce their kids to the
Internet and the online world. Kids'Crossing reviews
Web sites with the help of adult volunteers and provides a list of safe sites for younger kids. Despite the
heavy parental hand, it's still a cool hangout. You
can interact with other kids from all over the world
on the Lunchroom bulletin board. The Library helps
you with schoolwork, and the Computers area offers
tips for creating your own home page.

MIDLINK MAGAZINE
(http://longwood.cs.ucf.edu:80/~MidLink/)
Teacher Caroline McCullen, and her kids at Ligon
Middle School in Raleigh, North Carolina, do a great
job with this online 'zine for kids ages ten to fifteen.
It manages to be both fun and informative. You'll
find terrific student writing and electronic artwork.
There's also a good list of favorite Web pages chosen
by kids. *MidLink* is published on the web four times
each year: fall, winter, spring, and summer. Each
issue has a different theme. Contributions from other
kids and schools are welcome!

MR. EDIBLE STARCHY TUBER HEAD HOME PAGE
(http://winnie.acsu.buffalo.edu/potatoe/)
Call me cynical, but I have a sneaky suspicion this
used to be called the Mr. Potato Head Home Page
until the toy company Hasbro threatened to sue.

Maybe it's because there's a disclaimer on this page that says "Mr. Potato Head is a trademark and © 1995 Hasbro, Inc., Pawtucket, RI. All Rights Reserved." No biggie. I kinda like Mr. Edible Starchy Tuber Head better. This site is a lot of fun and a complete waste of time (we love that). Rearrange Mr. Edible Starchy Tuber Head's facial features via computer. Check out the PotatoCam—Dan Quayle's favorite Web site. Best feature: the Mr. Edible Starchy Tuber Head's Worst Nightmare page, in which you can learn to say, "Oh my god! There's an axe in my head!" in forty languages. (Spanish: *!Dios mio! !Hay una hacha en mi cabeza!*) Hmm. I wonder what's Japanese for "I have way too much time on my hands."

MTV ONLINE
(www.mtv.com)
If you want to visit MTV Online and see this site in all its intensely graphic splendor, log on when you wake up, point your browser at www.mtv.com, then go to school. Come home, have dinner, do some homework, watch an hour of TV. About the time you're ready to call it a day and hit the sack, all the artwork should be almost finished downloading. Once it's done, you'll find everything you could want about MTV: Buzz Clips, MTV News, 120 Minutes, VJ profiles, the Top 20, The Real World, Beavis and Butthead, and more.

THE NERDITY TEST
(http://www.vivanet.com/~ictx/nerd/index.htm)
Take this online quiz and answer questions about your education and schooling ("Do you sit in the front row in school more than twenty percent of the time?), computers ("Have you ever taken your com-

puter on vacation with you?"), clothing ("Does your underwear have your name in it?"), leisure time ("Can you name more than five shows on PBS?"), *Star Trek* ("Have you ever owned a pair of Spock ears?"), and other categories. To spend the time it would take to answer all *five hundred questions* in this quiz and get your nerdity rating, you'd really have to be a major-league—well, you know.

PEEPING TOM HOME PAGE
(http://www.ts.umu.se/~spaceman/camera.html)
Don't let the weird name fool you. It's actually a neat link to cameras that are wired to the Net. What's the weather like in New York City? With a mouse click, you can look at a live picture from the seventy-seventh floor of the Empire State Building. Click again, and you're looking through Beachcam, three thousand miles away in Santa Monica, California. Then go back across the country and check out the view from high above Niagara Falls. There are live outdoor views from all over the world—San Francisco, Maui, Scotland, Sweden, Australia—and dozens of others.

PIRANHACAM
(http://www.floater.com/strength/)
As you might guess from the name, this is a camera aimed at a tank full of flesh-eating piranhas. Not only can you look at the fish at a safe distance, you can read all kinds of fun facts about the piranhas. "They are fed twice a week. They seem to prefer earthworms, but are perfectly happy eating just about anything dropped in the tank," said their keeper. Does that include fingers? "I don't know if they would really try to eat fingers, since I have never

left my hand in the tank long enough to find out." Good idea.

PLANETWORKS
(http://www.canuck.com/Planet/index.html)
A cool site in which environmentally aware teens can express their views and concerns. The "electronic magazine with a conscience," Planet*works* is a place to publish stories, comics, inventions, "ecolizer" journalism, poetry, photography, and T-shirt designs on environmental issues. Almost all of the ideas on recycling and other green projects on this site were thought up by kids.

PLAYROOM
**(http://openweb.vassar.edu/students/
dohernandez/kids'corner/Playroom.html)**
Vassar college student Doris Hernandez is the person behind this cool jumping-off point to kids' sites on the Web. The indexes include Critters (Animals), Educational Fun, Homepages for kids, Books for Kids, Music, Toys, and more.

PLUGGED IN
(http://pebbles.pluggedin.org/)
Not every kid has his or her own computer at home. That's why Plugged In started an after-school Web hangout for children and families from low-income communities to learn how to use multimedia tools and design their own home pages. So, show some support and check out their cool projects!

REACT
(http://www.react.com/)
"The magazine where teens make news," *React* is dis-

tributed inside millions of newspapers across the United States every week. This virtual version features news, sports, entertainment, contests, jokes, and more.

THE REALLY BIG BUTTON THAT DOESN'T DO ANYTHING
(http://www.wam.umd.edu/~twoflowr/button.htm)
Just what it says. Really. No Kidding. Don't ask.

REVERSE LINK
(http://www.io.org/~sward/Overview/html)
This site is the brainchild of sixteen-year-old Robin Ward of Toronto, who says, "It seems that everywhere you go on the Web, the information you find is totally useless. Well, this page isn't that bad, it's *worse*. The difference is that our stuff doesn't suck." Check this site for cool links to comics, sci-fi, music sites, and other stuff that, well, doesn't suck.

SPLASH KIDS
(http://www.splash.com)
Splash Kids is described by the Cybernet Company, which runs this site, as "a place where kids can come to play games, expand their minds, and make new friends." Cool features include What's Hot/What's Not in different countries around the world, Virtual School for field trips via modem, an online art gallery of kids' art, a Grab Bag of jokes updated every day, links to game sites, chat and message boards, Tech Talk about computers and the Internet, and lots more. You can also register to win a Sony Discman and other monthly prizes.

THE TEENAGE LOUNGE
(http://yourtown.com/teen/lounge/)

"The home of teens in cyberspace," this page was put up by a thirteen-year-old kid who calls himself Eric of the Web. Any teenager in cyberspace can become a member of Teenage Lounge. Kids from all over the United States and other countries have cruised by the lounge, leaving little biographical sketches and e-mail addresses. You'll also find links to other great kids' sites.

THE TEENAGER'S CIRCLE- - - - - - - - - - - - -
(http://www.exclamation.com/teencircle/)

One of the coolest things about life on the Net is that it's just as easy to make friends around the world as in your neighborhood or school. When you're online the world *is* your neighborhood.

A terrific example of this is the Teenager's Circle, a group of seven online friends in the United States, Malaysia, England, and Latvia, who work together on online projects for other teenagers.

Want your own home page on the Web? One Teenager's Circle project is **BHI Teens** 90210 (http://www.asiaconnect. com.my/90210/), which provides free personal home pages for teenagers. It doesn't even matter if you know hypertext markup language (HTML). Just type out the exact text you want to have on your home page, and they'll covert it into HTML format for you.

BHI Teens is a real Web success story. It's been designated one of the "top 5 percent of all websites" by Point Communications, and it's won a bunch of other awards. The site's creator, Gerald Tan Chuang Win, a student at Penang Free School in Malaysia, was even featured in the big "24 Hours in Cyberspace" event last February (http://www.cyber24.com).

"I think in the near future, the Internet will not be a luxury but a necessity to both kids and adults," said Gerald, a fourteen-year-old Web pioneer who is working hard with his friends to make that happen. Note to Bill Gates: watch your back, pal!

Gerald logged onto the Internet for the first time in the fall of 1995 and learned HTML online. "I was so happy when I finally got my Web page set up. I wanted other teenagers to feel the same, too. That's why I help them to set up pages." The result was BHI Teens. "Soon, a lot of people were excited about this project," said Gerald via e-mail from Malaysia, "and they wanted to help me on it."

Among those helping out in the early days was Najah Onn, who lives several hours north of Gerald in Kuala Lumpur, Malaysia. Najah began surfing the Web in October 1995. "One day, when I was surfing around, I found BHI Teens, and I thought it would be wonderful to have a home page, said Najah Onn. "I was impressed that Gerald was from Malaysia, because I am too! Unfortunately, I lived in Kuala Lumpur, and Gerald lived in Penang Island, somewhere north."

Najah began trading e-mail with Gerald. "He said that he wanted to put up a club with people around the globe joining it," said Najah. "He asked me if I wanted to be the marketing director, so I agreed!" Web development director Corinne Seaton and Web resources director Joseph Volence, two fifteen-year-old American teenagers who run their own online bulletin board, were the next recruits. Next came seventeen-year-old Andris Kalinka of Latvia, now the vice president of Teenagers Circle. His job is maintaining all the home pages BHI Teens puts up.

In addition to BHI Teens, The Teenager's Circle gives out the Thumbs-up Award to other Web sites created by or for teens and kids. "We work on projects together," said Gerald, "which we hope will make the Internet a better place for kids and teenagers."

Daniel Peters, eleven, is the youngest member of the Teenager's Circle, but having been online since July 1995, he's the veteran Net surfer of the group. Daniel learned HTML from friends and on his own. He's the technical director of BHI Teens and the coordinator with Najah of Thumbs-up! Rounding out Teenager's Circle is Matt Swoboda, a fifteen-year-old English teenager who is the editor of *90210 Teen Zone,* the biweekly newsletter.

You can check out the projects the Teenager's Circle is working on at:

BHI TEENS 90210
  (http://www.asiaconnect.com.my/90210)

The Thumbs-up! Award
  (http://www.exclamation.com/teencircle/thumbsup)

The 90210 Teenzone
  (http://www.exclamation.com/teencircle/teenzone)

Teenagers Circle Mailing List
  (http://www.exclamation.com/teencircle/maillist)

"Eventually, the Internet will be so common that almost everyone will have access to it," said Gerald, "just like the telephone we have everywhere. I believe that the Internet is the first true global communications medium and marketplace at the same time."

- -

THE TEEN PAGE
(http://www.1starnet.com/teen)
Webmaster Brian Rhea does an amazing job keeping his page stocked with up-to-date links to the latest movies, television shows, sport sites, humor, etc.

TEENVILLE, USA
(http://www.exclamation.com/teenville/index.html)
Nothing fancy ... simply a place on the WWW for teens to have fun. Teenville is currently looking for intelligent teens to help out with planning and up-dating future projects for Teenville. Links are provided to fun sites, music sites, and teen sites, with movie and sports links in the works.

THREADS
(http://www.jayi.com/sbi/Threads/opent.html)
A message board for teenagers to create and discuss topics, or Chunks—their name for the "big areas of life." Chunks? Threads? What's with these guys? It's still a cool place to talk with other kids all over the world about technology, school, relationships, whatever.

A TRIP THROUGH THE GRAND CANYON
(http://river.ihs.gov/GrandCanyon/GCrt.html)
Take a trip through the Grand Canyon and look at pictures and maps of the different spots along the route.

THE ULTIMATE BAND LIST
(http://american.recordings.com/wwwofmusic/ubl/ubl.shtml)
The name says it all. It's the Web's largest interactive

list of music links. Thousands of bands, thousands of links. A must-see for music fans.

THE VIRTUAL DORM
(http://www.taponline.com/tap/v-dorm.html)
It's *90210* for the cyberspace crowd! This is a cyber-drama-sitcom set in a college dorm.

TV1
(http://tv1.com/wot/index.html)
What's on TV tonight? At this site you can customize TV listings for your time zone, view listings up to six days in advance, search listings by key words—you can even create your own personalized TV listings based on your interests.

WE DIDN'T START THE FIRE
(http://users.aol.com/jdsweeney/fire.html)
This doesn't really qualify as a Web site, but it's still pretty clever. AOL member J. D. Sweeney created a hypertext document with the lyrics to Billy Joel's "We Didn't Start the Fire." The entire song is basically a laundry list of historical events since the 1950s, and Sweeney has hot-linked nearly every word in the song to a Web source that tells you more about who or what the song is talking about. An amazing creative use of hypertext!

WWW SPIROGRAPH
(http://juniper.tc.cornell.edu:8000/spiro/
spiro.html)
An online version of the Spirograph toy, which draws intricate patterns with rotating wheels. In the actual toy, you place a colored pen in a hole in a plastic disk that goes inside a flat plastic ring. When

you push the disk around the inside edge of the ring, beautiful, elaborate designs are created. For the online version, no pen is required—simply enter the radii of the ring and the circle, as well as how far the pen is placed from the edge of the circle. Did I say "simply"? Never mind. It's easier than it sounds, and lots of fun.

ZOILUS
(http://pages.prodigy.com/MD/zoilus/zoilus1.html)

An unusual online 'zine by teens in Gaithersburg, Maryland. In their own words: "The truth about high school—friends. Friday nights. Football games. Dropouts. Disillusionment. Regret. What does high school mean to you? Are these four years really the best years of our lives? We asked ourselves what high school means to us, five students, each halfway into our senior, and hopefully last, year of high school. What we discovered will most likely not lift anyone's spirits or give anyone a comfortable view of high school, but it will, we hope, shed some new light on the modern day high school experience and provide some insight into what it's like to be an adolescent in the 1990s."

CHECK THESE OUT!

Aha! Kids Network
   (http://www.aha-kids.com/)

ESPNET Sports Zone
   (http://espnet.sportszone.com/index.text.html)

Girl Games
   (http://www.sccsi.com/girlgames)

Girls InterWire
(http://www.sccsi.com/girlgames/interwire.html)

Happy Puppy Games
(http://happypuppy.com/)

Internet@Night: Not Just for Kids!
(http://www.night.net/kids)

Kids on the Web
(http://www.zen.org/~brendan/kids.html)

Kids' Web
(http://www.primenet.com/~sburr/index.html)

Nucleus Kids' Page
(http://www.nucleus.com/kids.html)

Oasis Kids' Corner
(http://www.ot.com/kids/)

Rachel's Place
(http://www.mcs.net/~kathyw/fun.html)

Sylvans' KidSpace
(http://remarque.berkeley.edu/~tigger/kids.html)

The Internet Movie Database
(http://www.msstate.edu/movies/)

The Ultimate Children's Internet Sites
(http://www.vividus.com/ucis.html)

Tic-Tac-Toe
(http://www.bu.edu/games/tictactoe)

TV Net
(http://www.tvnet.com/)

Uncle Bob's Kids' Page
(http://gagme.wwa.com/~boba/kids.html)

Unofficial Pez Home Page
(http://wwwcsif.cs.ucdavis.edu/~telford/pez.html)

Web Comics
  (http://www.cyberzine.com/webcomics/)

Web World
  (http://sailfish.peregrine.com/WebWorld/
  welcome.html)

Weird Al Yankovic Lyrics
  (http://crist1.see.plym.ac.uk/dfsmith/index.html)

World Wide Web of Sports
  (http://www.tns.lcs.mit.edu/cgi-bin/sports)

Zarf's List of Interactive Games on the Web
  (http://www.leftfoot.com/games.html)

Index